St Elizabeth's
L

Dealing with sick kids can be heartbreaking,
funny, and uplifting, often all at once!

This series takes a look at a hospital set up
especially to deal with such children,
peeping behind the scenes into almost all the
departments and clinics, exploring the
problems and solutions of various diseases,
while watching the staff fall helplessly
in love—with the kids and with each other.

Enjoy!

Abigail Gordon is fascinated by words, and what better way to use them than in the crafting of romance between the sexes—a state of the heart that has affected almost everyone at some time in their lives? Twice widowed, she now lives alone in a Cheshire village. Her two eldest sons between them have presented her with three delightful grandchildren, and her youngest son lives nearby.

Recent titles by the same author:

MORRISON'S MAGIC

ABIGAIL GORDON

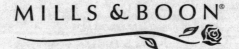

MILLS & BOON®

First published in Great Britain 2000
Harlequin Mills & Boon Limited,
Eton House, 18-24 Paradise Road, Richmond, Surrey TW9 1SR

© Abigail Gordon 2000

ISBN 0 263 82432 2

Set in Times Roman 10½ on 12 pt.
112-0009-51823

Printed and bound in Spain
by Litografia Rosés S.A., Barcelona

CHAPTER ONE

CLAUDIA was met by the pale rays of a February sun as she emerged at street level from the concrete compound that was St Elizabeth's underground car park.

Briefcase in hand and with her long beige wool coat wrapped tightly around her, she shivered in the cold morning air, thinking as she did so that she never felt warm these days and it wasn't entirely due to the time of year.

Yet chilled though she may be, there was no urge in her to go straight inside the structure that had once been the centre of her existence.

Crossing over the busy road, she stood on the opposite pavement and observed the huge grey stone building that was St Elizabeth's Children's Hospital, one of the country's most famous centres of paediatric care.

A place where some of the top medical brains of the country cared for small sufferers with dedication and zeal. There had always been the feeling of being part of a great band of carers when she'd worked there before and no doubt it would still be the same.

As Claudia continued to gaze upon the famous hospital she found herself straightening her shoulders, wetting cold lips, and tightening her grip on the case in her hand.

Coming back to Lizzie's had seemed the obvious answer when she'd finally surfaced from the strange limbo that she'd been in for so many months, but at this moment she wasn't so sure.

The junior doctor who was about to present herself to Personnel within a matter of minutes, before making her way to the orthopaedic unit, was a very different person from the carefree high-flyer who had left the hospital almost a year ago to travel around the world with a cherished companion.

Now she was back…and dithering…which didn't fit in with the veneer of brittle confidence she had adopted since coming back to England.

'Get in there,' she told herself firmly. 'Stop hesitating. Show them that Claudy's back in town.'

When a break in the traffic came she took her own advice, crossed over, and went in.

Nothing had changed. Mrs Lewis, sporting what looked like a recent perm, was making up a basket of fruit in Dunwoody in the entrance hall as Claudia had seen her do countless times before. Engrossed in her task, she didn't see the lissom young doctor stride past.

But white-haired Mr Goode did from behind the counter of the hospital's small post office and he called out to her, eager to know in what guise she was back at Lizzie's.

There was no response and he thought that either young Dr Craven hadn't heard him, or else she was pretending she hadn't. Whatever the reason, she was out of sight in seconds, leaving him none the wiser.

He'd chatted with her sometimes in the staff restaurant or when she'd popped in for stamps, before she'd gone gallivanting off on some hare-brained sort of prolonged holiday that he'd decided was either a working vacation…or evidence that a certain young doctor didn't have to rely on her hospital pay.

Anyway, wherever she'd been, and for whatever reason, she was back, and no doubt the answer to his surmisings would soon be revealed if hospital gossip ran true to form.

Having verified with Personnel that she was indeed back on the payroll of St Elizabeth's and expected to present herself on the orthopaedic wards forthwith, Claudia headed for the lift that would take her to familiar surroundings.

There were a couple of nurses in the lift when it came, a cleaner, and an elderly consultant resplendent in black jacket and pinstriped trousers, who was reading his mail and holding a bulging leather briefcase.

Claudia met the tentative smiles of the nurses with a brief one of her own and stood back in the corner to await take-off.

As the lift doors began to close a man appeared from nowhere and catapulted himself inside with the agility of a mountain cat—and the same ferocity.

'Morning, Colin,' he growled in the direction of the dark-suited consultant who was eyeing him in some surprise over his glasses. 'Some idiot has parked their "cult car" where I usually put mine and I've been circling around for ages trying to find a place!'

'Cult car?' the other man questioned mildly.

'Yes,' the athletic-looking complainant growled. 'There's a red Porsche Boxter down there amongst the staff cars. It puts your Merc into the shade, I can tell you!'

The other man laughed. 'If that's the case *your* battered old banger won't stand a chance. I keep telling you that you're depriving the scrap heap.'

'Gets me where I want to go,' Colin was told in a slightly less tetchy tone. 'There are too many poseurs about in the motoring world for my liking.'

Claudia had listened mutinously to the conversation. It had to be her car that the dark-haired stranger, dressed in a black high-necked sweater and grey trousers, was referring to.

He was an exotic-looking man with dark brows above keen eyes, high cheek-bones, a mouth that looked as if smiles sat on it rarely, and a taut jaw-line that spoke of purpose…and arrogance maybe.

Whatever it was, she was in no mood to hear herself described as a 'poseur' just because this ranting Mephistopheles had got out of the wrong side of the bed.

'The Boxter belongs to me,' she said coolly, 'and as there was no indication to say that the space belonged to anyone in particular, I saw nothing wrong in parking there.

'I'm sorry if my choice of vehicle doesn't meet with your approval. Maybe you're of the opinion that hospital staff should transport themselves in go-carts or on roller blades.'

When she'd started to speak the irate man had swivelled round to where Claudia was standing erect and haughty at the back of the lift, and as his fiery gaze met the cool blue of her own one of the nurses giggled, while the other shuffled uncomfortably, and the consultant sighed as if he could do without this sort of thing at eight-thirty in the morning.

If the man had been about to reply he didn't get the chance. At that moment the lift swished to a halt and, leaving the others behind, he and Claudia stepped out onto a corridor that was signposted 'ORTHOPAEDIC WARDS'.

'So you're staff?' he said in the same tone that he might have used to say, 'So you've got something catching?'

'Yes, that's right,' she said. 'I'm about to take up where I left off as a doctor on the orthopaedics section. And who are you? Apart from being a first-class whinger?'

His smile had the cold brilliance of an iceberg. 'Lucas Morrison, head of that same unit.'

Claudia's insides did a somersault but she gave no sign of it. At present there was little joy in each day as it came and, having now met the man she would be working with, today looked as if it was going to be joyless in the extreme.

But it would take more than an arrogant Mr Pushy to get through *her* armour, and with that thought in mind she pointed herself towards the closed doors of the nearest ward.

Unabashed he fell in step beside her and, as if he just couldn't give up on his earlier waspishness, said brusquely, 'So what's your name?'

He was some bossy-boots! She could imagine how a young probationer would feel if they got this kind of reception from a senior member of staff.

'Little Bo Peep,' she said sweetly, with a feeling that she was going to be on a disciplinary before she'd even taken her coat off.

'I think not. You're the wrong type. She was a meek little thing. How about Claudia Craven…the jet-setting doctor? She's the one I've been told to expect.'

'You got me there, Guv'nor. I'll come clean,' she told him with her hand on the door handle. 'Yes, I am she. Claudia Craven, back in harness once more, instead of lazing on tropical beaches.'

His lip was curling as they went through the door together, and Claudia could tell that this guy had already judged her before she'd even shown her face. What had he heard about her? And how was she going to work in harmony with someone like him?

He'd been irritable from the moment of entering the lift for some reason and, in fairness, she hadn't improved matters with her own attitude, but, really, who did he think he was?

She was about to find out.

By the time she'd taken off her outdoor things and hung them in the staff room, introduced herself to plump, auburn-haired, Jess Richardson, the sister in charge, and pinned the name-tag that was waiting for her onto her smart blouse, Lucas Morrison had already done his ward round and was waiting with thinly veiled impatience for her introductions to the rest of the staff to be completed before he took her over.

'How rusty are you?' was his first question. 'You've been away from medicine for almost a year, I'm told.'

There were a couple of smart back answers to that too, but she wasn't going to venture them. For one thing he wouldn't have a clue what she was on about if she were to tell him that she'd been closer to medical care than she'd ever been during the past year, and that if the wetness of tears caused rust she should be covered in it.

'Yes, I know I have, but I don't forget things easily,' she told him confidently, thinking that life would be so much easier if she did. 'I may have to read up on some things that aren't as clear in my mind as they were previously, but basically I'm hoping to carry on where I left off.'

He raised a dubious eyebrow. 'Hmm. We'll see. It's to be hoped that the high life hasn't made you soft. A doctor's life is not an easy one.'

'I'm aware of that,' she replied stonily. 'I *have* worked on the wards before.'

What was the matter with the man? If gloom and doom were his stock in trade he must be a riot with his young patients!

How Lucas Morrison treated his patients was about to be revealed and it was vastly different from the way he'd been dealing with her.

Jess Richardson, the sister in charge, was approaching from the other end of the ward. 'Lucas, Michael Sutton is complaining that the leg frame is hurting,' she said.

'We've done all we can to make it as comfortable as possible, but he isn't very happy.'

'I'll have a word with him, Sister,' he said immediately, and as he moved towards a bed at the far end of the ward he looked over his shoulder and clicked his fingers at Claudia, following the gesture with a brisk, 'Well, come along, then, Dr Craven. You *are* here to assist me.'

Which was quite correct. She was. But was she the only one? Surely she and Lucas Morrison weren't the only doctors serving Orthopaedics?

It transpired that the abrasive orthopaedic surgeon had done an external fixation of a broken tibia the previous day and its youthful recipient was complaining of pain from the surgery, which had consisted of fixing a metal frame with long pins attached to it on his leg.

The positioning of the frame had been done in such a way that the pins penetrated through the skin and into the fractured bone, a procedure that would hold the damaged tibia in position while it healed.

In a couple of days the young patient would be discharged and his parents would take over the manipulation of the frame by tightening it to a further degree each day.

Claudia had seen it done before in place of the usual plaster cast and knew of its success, but she also knew that it could be painful and was not surprised to hear that in this instance it was.

'What's up, Mikey?' asked the man who had led the way to the ten-year-old's bed with brisk strides. 'Hurting, is it?'

'Yes, Doctor,' the lad sobbed. 'I want to go home.'

The dark-haired doctor bent down and took the boy's hand in his. 'You *are* going home…soon,' he told him gently, 'but that won't stop it from hurting. Sister is going to give you some nice medicine to stop the pain and in a little while it should feel better. Is that OK?'

'If you say so, Doctor,' Mikey said forlornly as he wiped away the tears with the back of his hand.

'So, what do *you* think of this method of treating a fracture?' Lucas Morrison asked as they left the boy to the sister's ministrations.

Claudia shrugged and knew immediately that the gesture had irritated him.

'I think it is a vast improvement in the right situation. It saves the patient being encased in plaster for weeks on end.'

She was grappling with the situation in which she found herself. It was incredible that she had no sooner shown her face at Lizzie's than she was being commandeered by this human tornado. Hadn't he got anything better to do?

So far, apart from Mrs Lewis down on Dunwoody and Mr Goode in the post office, who had spotted her the moment she'd entered the hospital, she hadn't met a single person she knew.

She'd expected to find at least one or two of the staff who'd been there before, but it looked as if the board had been swept clean on Orthopaedics and the fellow who was in charge was the biggest unknown quantity of all.

The year before last Anthony Bellingham had been the top man in the orthopaedics section but he had been approaching retirement. Maybe that was the reason for the 'new broom'.

In her present state of mind the last thing Claudia wanted was confrontation of any kind, but she had a shrewd suspicion that this man thrived on it and, much as she longed for peace, there was no way that she was going to allow him to trample all over her.

He'd been lovely with the boy, though, and she supposed that should be enough—and if his bolshie attitude got the best results from his staff, what was the problem?

The problem was that it wasn't going to work with her. They might be at opposite ends of the health-care ladder but he must have been a junior doctor once. Although such was his brisk arrogance it was hard to believe that he could have ever been anything but 'top dog'.

His accent was that of the true northerner, while hers was Surrey at its most refined. This Lucas Morrison no doubt thought that the car went with the accent, but then *he* wasn't to know that it was a gift from her father.

It was Charles Craven's most recent attempt to banish the despair that had held his daughter in its grip ever since she'd come home with a golden tan, a tangled mass of sun-bleached hair...and a shattered dream.

Yet the dream had been shattered long before that. It had splintered on the day that the oncologist had told Jack how long he'd got, and it was when the prophet of doom had left his bedside that the lanky, marine biologist had said, 'All right, Claudia. So I'm not going to live to a ripe old age. Let's make the most of what time I've got left, shall we?'

When he'd explained what he'd meant by that she'd stared at him in stunned surprise, but only for a second, and then she'd held him close and whispered, 'Anything. Anything at all if it makes you happy. I'll give in my notice tomorrow.'

'I'm due in theatre in a few minutes,' Lucas Morrison was saying, 'so in the meantime I suggest that you familiarise yourself with the youngsters who have come to us for help, and get to know the staff and the ward routine.'

Claudia nodded as relief swept over her. He was going to disappear. Thank God! Surely he didn't give every new member of staff the sort of grilling he'd given her? But then every newcomer didn't arrive in a scarlet Porsche Boxter.

He would be surprised to know that in her present state of mind the car featured as merely a means of transport. Admittedly it wouldn't have been like that at one time. She would have been over the moon to have the keys of such a dream buggy put into her hand, but she'd learned the hard way that money couldn't buy the things that really mattered...such as good health...life itself.

'I believe you've just come back from a round-the-world trip,' Jess, the ward sister, said when he'd gone. 'That must have cost a packet.'

'Yes, it did,' Claudia agreed. It *had* cost a lot...in more ways than one, but the topic wasn't up for discussion. Not as far as she was concerned, anyway.

'You must be loaded,' another voice said from behind, and she turned to find a middle-aged staff nurse, who had been introduced to her as Sheila Newcome, eyeing her frostily.

'I still have to work for my living,' Claudia told her, taken aback at the unexpected censure from a stranger.

'When you feel like it,' the other woman said sneeringly. 'Some of us are lucky if we get a day at the seaside, and now *you've* come swanning back here as if you own the place.'

Claudia's smile was mocking. 'Maybe I do. You'd better watch your step,' and with a glance at the auburn-haired sister, she added, 'I'd be obliged if you could put me in the picture regarding the children's problems.'

Jess Richardson nodded and without speaking led the way to the nearest bed.

Aware that the chill was still in the air Claudia said from behind, 'Maybe if I caught the bus tomorrow...and stopped off at the charity shop for a change of wardrobe, I might be received more cordially, do you think?'

She watched the back of the ward sister's neck redden and felt ashamed that she was meeting waspishness with waspishness. It was barely an hour since she'd arrived at the one place where she was hoping to find some sense of purpose and it was all going wrong.

But as they moved from bed to bed Claudia's world righted itself. This was what it was all about: the young ones who needed them, desperately in some cases. Their parents had entrusted them to Lizzie's and would not be expecting them to be in the midst of personality clashes and petty jealousies.

As the sister escorted her around the ward, giving a brief outline of each child's illness and pausing while Claudia glanced through their notes, both women were putting all other thoughts to one side.

'This is Charlotte,' Jess Richardson said when they stopped beside the cot of a tiny baby girl, and with a smile for the child's mother. 'Neonatal screening showed a hip abnormality and she was passed on to us.'

Claudia nodded as she leafed through the baby's notes. 'Yes, I see. Lucas Morrison states that she has a congenital dislocation of the hip.'

'That's right. He's seen her in Outpatients and then had her brought in a couple of days ago for observation before he decides whether to put the little mite in a splint,' the ward sister said.

'Quite so,' Claudia agreed. 'It's not always easy to decide what to do in these cases. I saw a few unstable hips when I was here before and the problem is that some of those revealed in the screening process resolve spontaneously while others develop into a completely dislocated hip. There is no doubt that splinting prevents any permanent dislocation and I suppose that is what he has in mind.'

'Lucas never takes any chances,' the sister said in tones that were bordering on reverence. 'He lives and breathes Lizzie's. He saw Charlotte just after they'd found the defect and asked to see her again at four months, which is now. She's going to have a pelvic X-ray today to check the position of the femoral heads and from that he'll decide whether to use splinting.'

A curly-haired boy in the next bed was watching them with wary eyes and when they moved on to him he got the first word in.

'Are you a new doctor?' he asked. 'I haven't seen you before.'

'Sort of,' she told him with a smile. 'I've worked here once before and have come back to help Dr Morrison and the other doctors.'

'What's your name?'

'Claudia…or my friends call me "Claudy".'

'Can I call you that?'

'Of course…and what do I call you?'

'This is Joshua,' Jess Richardson said, ruffling the boy's dark curls. 'He's seven years old and a regular little gasbag. Josh has Perthes' disease. He came to Lizzie's with a pronounced limp and pain in top of his leg.

'We've found that there is some wasting of the quadriceps muscle above the knee and X-rays have shown erosion of the head of the right femoral growing area.

'Lucas has ordered bedrest for a few weeks and then he's going to splint the hip to relieve pressure on the femur.'

'Does Lucas prefer to be called by his first name?' Claudia questioned casually. 'Most consultants don't encourage it.'

The other woman laughed. 'They're not him. There's no side to Lucas Morrison. That one is a law unto himself. All he cares about is the job.'

'Yes, I see,' Claudia murmured thoughtfully.

That he was a law unto himself she'd already discovered. For the rest of it she would pass judgement when she'd seen a bit more of the man.

In the late afternoon Claudia was on the ward signing a prescription for a child about to be discharged, when for the first time since arriving she heard a familiar voice and, turning towards where her name was being called in tones of pleased surprise, she saw Belinda Brown approaching with hands outstretched.

'Where have *you* sprung from, Claudy?' the chubby medical secretary cried as she gave her an affectionate squeeze. 'You're the last person I'd expected to see in Lizzie's.'

'I'm back, Belinda,' she informed the only member of staff who had any idea why she'd gone off on a trip round the world with the man she was going to marry.

The other woman's eyes had clouded. 'And Jack?'

Claudia shrugged and the gesture had a bleak finality about it. 'Gone.'

'Oh! I'm so sorry.'

'It was always on the cards,' she said sombrely, 'but none the less painful when it came.'

'I can imagine,' Belinda said with a quick look round to make sure they weren't being overheard. 'And now you're back in harness.'

'Yes, and so far am not exactly getting the returned prodigal treatment. The fatted calf has been replaced with a pushy censorious consultant and nurses who think I'm

some kind of rich bitch playing at doctors. All because I
came in a flashy car!'

Belinda was smiling at the droll comparisons. 'Obviously they don't know you. Two of the nurses that you
worked with before are still here, Maggie and Kate, but it
must be their day off…and, although Lucas Morrison *is*
somewhat overpowering, he's the best we've ever had. He
and I get on fine. I smooth out the admin problems and he
straightens the bones.

'If he's seeing you in the same light as the nurses are
and is not impressed, it's probably because he's the boy
from the run-down council estate who only got where he
is with a lot of hard graft.'

Claudia pulled a wry face. 'I thought that class consciousness was a thing of the past. I didn't ask to be born
the child of wealthy parents any more than Jack did…and,
in any case, Mum and Dad are the ones with the money—
not me. They're very generous and supportive, especially
now, but I have to find my own way, Belinda, and since
I came back to England it's been really hard.'

'You poor, sweet thing,' her friend said softly. 'Why
don't you let me tell the folks here what you're going
through?'

Claudia shook her head. 'No. If they can't like me for
what I am without my having to play on their sympathy,
it's just too bad.'

If Belinda had any comment to make about that she was
forestalled by the arrival of Lucas Morrison on the ward
once more, and this time Claudia saw him in a different
light.

Not that she liked him any more. There was an explo-
sive sort of toughness about this urban tiger that made her
wary of him, but she supposed that he had to be admired.

Even with a full grant it wasn't easy to get through

medical school. The odds were that he'd had to get a job as well and, with reams of facts and figures to plough through and career experience on the wards, a medical student's life was far from being a joyride.

He was watching her with bright, observant eyes and Claudia tilted her chin. The day was nearly over. Soon she would go back to her silent flat in a smart London suburb and, for once, instead of the quietness of it crowding in on her, she would be grateful to be on her own, away from the ripples that she seemed to have created on her return to Lizzie's.

Meeting up with Belinda again had been good...very good. Lucas Morrison's secretary was a pleasant, likeable woman with a loving husband and teenage twins. Altogether a combination to be envied, but there were other aspects of the day that she wasn't so sure about and the man who was about to inflict himself on her once more was mostly to blame for that.

'Well, Claudia Craven. How's it gone?' he wanted to know.

She eyed him levelly. 'All right, thank you, Mr Morrison.'

The formal manner of her reply was meant to annoy...and it did. She could tell by the way his mouth became a tight line, but if he wanted to be everyone else's friend he wasn't going to be hers.

'The name is Lucas,' he was informing her edgily. 'I don't stand on ceremony. We on Orthopaedics are a team, each with our role to play, understood?'

'Yes, *sir*,' she mocked, and wondered why she was letting him get under her skin to such an extent, and then, reverting to seriousness, she asked the question that had been on her lips all day but hadn't been asked.

He was glowering at her flippant approach to his description of the work of the unit and his expression didn't change much when she said, 'Where are the other doctors in Orthopaedics? Surely we're not the only ones?'

'Of course not. We had Paula Conrad as registrar, but she's moved on and we don't have a replacement yet. Then we have Miles Soper, who is a sick man at the moment and only attends when he's well enough…and the boy wonder, Robin Crawshaw, on the same level as yourself.

'Outpatients have their own orthopaedic team, which takes some of the burden off us, but we don't have much time to hang around.'

He was aware that it was time for her to go and as she went to put on the long beige coat he followed her. 'Zooming off home now, are we…in the Boxter?'

'That's right. And you're going to be doing likewise in your old banger, I suppose?'

There was irony in the smile he bestowed on her. 'No. I live in staff accommodation here at the hospital.'

That surprising piece of information filled her with questions, but to Lucas Morrison there must have been only one that he expected to hear and he was ready with the answer.

'My parking problems this morning were because I'd been away for the weekend.'

Later that evening Claudia stood in the flat that she was renting and looked around her. So far she hadn't taken much notice of it.

It was elegant, expensive, and might just as well have been a mud hut for all she cared. But after the comments she'd received on the orthopaedic unit earlier in the day, she was seeing it in a new light.

She supposed it went with the car and would no doubt be commented on to that effect if any of those she was going to be working with saw it. But the chances of that happening were slim. She lived in a neighbourhood that would be above most of their incomes, except in the case of Lucas Morrison.

A thought which brought to mind what he'd said with regard to *his* accommodation. It was most unusual for a consultant of his standing to be occupying one of the hospital's flatlets.

Was he trying to prove something? she wondered. In fact, were they both trying to prove something? He, that position and prestige meant nothing to him, and she, that the wealth to which she'd always been accustomed was of little importance—when the reason for living had been taken away.

In the silence of the luxurious rooms the sights and sounds of those strange months in limbo came back once again to torment her. She found herself gripping the back of a chair, her eyes closed against the tears that she couldn't hold back.

They'd been in India when it had happened. Memories of remote villages where livestock scampered in the dust…the taste of thirst-quenching mango juice…the constant heat…were mixed up with the babble of Anjuna's weekly flea market held beside a golden beach.

There'd been hundreds of stalls, performing artists, bullocks draped in silks and jewels, body-piercing taking place in shabby tents, and above it all the heavy aroma of hashish.

The noise had been deafening, but later…much later…as they'd sat in a deserted corner of the beach, there had been no sound as Jack had keeled over and she'd watched the bright red tide pumping out of him onto the golden sand.

Claudia had known it had to come, but there had been no one to tell her exactly when would be the time, or where would be the place.

CHAPTER TWO

THE next morning Claudia resisted the urge to seek out the previous day's parking spot and used the first empty space that presented itself, but it didn't stop her from checking to see who was parked there.

To her surprise the place was empty. So it didn't look as if Lucas Morrison had made haste to claim it for himself the moment she'd left for home the previous night, which was rather surprising after he'd made such a fuss.

But there were more important things to be considering than that, she told herself as she walked quickly into the glass-covered entrance hall of the hospital. Such as what the day would bring on the wards.

Would she receive a warmer welcome than yesterday? Was she going to be monopolised again by the man who seemed to have the rest of the staff drooling over him? Would the two young staff nurses that Belinda had mentioned be in today? She would soon know.

The attitude of the sister in charge and Sheila Newcome was just as lacking in cordiality as on the previous day, but a young doctor perched on the corner of the desk in the ward office seemed happy enough to see her.

'You must be Claudia Craven,' he said, eyeing her approvingly as he slid off the desk and stood in front of her, a slim, white-coated figure with long brown hair and light hazel eyes.

'Yes, I am,' she told him with a wary smile and waited for him to introduce himself, even though his youth and the name-tag he was displaying made it unnecessary. Here was Robin Crawshaw, described by Lucas Morrison as the 'boy wonder'.

'Robin Crawshaw,' he said, shaking hands with undisguised enthusiasm. 'I've heard a lot about you and am very pleased to make your acquaintance.'

Out of the corner of her eye Claudia saw the ward sister and Sheila Newcome exchange glances. 'Likewise,' she said pleasantly. 'It's nice to know that there's at least one person who isn't prepared to prejudge me.'

She noted that he didn't question the comment. Which meant that he was aware that her return to Lizzie's had received a lukewarm reception from everyone except her friend, Belinda Brown.

As if to give extra substance to that depressing thought, the two young staff nurses that Claudia had worked with previously appeared on the ward at that moment, one of them pushing the drugs trolley and the other with a pile of clean bed linen in her arms.

They glanced across at the office and then looked away and Claudia got the message. So far, the only member of the medical staff who seemed pleased to see her was this likeable young doctor.

Maybe he was of the opinion that if *he* got the chance to fly off into the unknown for months on end he would do the same. She hoped it would be for a different reason from her own if he ever did.

The person whose disapproval she felt the most hadn't put in an appearance so far and she was grateful for his absence. As with a strong and bitter medicine, she would prefer to receive him in small doses.

In the meantime there were young patients to see, their progress reports to read through, and the latest arrival to examine once the nursing staff had settled her into the ward.

Eight-year-old Holly Yates had been involved in a car crash the previous evening and had suffered fractures of the ankle and both arms.

From Accident and Emergency she had been taken straight to X-ray and from there to theatre, where, according to what they were saying on the ward, Lucas Morrison had operated on the child in the early hours of the morning.

He had inserted screws across the bone ends to immobilise an unstable ankle fracture, and repositioned the broken bones in her arms by means of open reduction, and now, with the injured limbs in plaster casts, she was being admitted to the orthopaedic unit, still very shocked and weepy.

Holly's distraught parents, who had both escaped unhurt from the crash, were walking beside the trolley as she was wheeled into the ward. From what they were saying it seemed that they were each blaming the other for the injuries their daughter had received.

Her mother was berating her father for not making sure that the child had her seat belt fastened and he was castigating her because she'd been rushing him to get her to line dancing on time.

As Claudia was about to point out that it was too late for recriminations and they should be concentrating on Holly instead of arguing, someone else stepped in to do it for her.

'Listening to you both snarling at each other isn't doing your daughter any good,' Lucas Morrison said suddenly from behind. 'If you're going to carry on like this you'd better leave the ward. We have other youngsters here who are far from well and I don't want them upset by your behaviour.'

Claudia hid a smile. Lucas was running true to form, but on this occasion he had her full support.

The overwrought couple trailed off into silence at the brisk rebuke from the man who had operated on their daughter and stood side by side watching the nurses lift Holly onto the bed.

'Why people can't accept the knocks that life hands out to them with a bit more grace is beyond me,' Lucas Morrison said in a low voice as they moved away to allow the nurses time to settle the injured child.

Claudia's eyes were bleak as she turned her head away. What would he say about the way *she* was coping with the worst 'knock' of all—if he knew? Would he be impressed—or scornful because she was finding it so hard?

It was something that she wasn't likely to find out, as there was no way she was going to pour her heart out to anyone at Lizzie's...least of all the urban tiger himself.

'Do I hear the voice of someone who has had his share of life's problems?' she asked with what she hoped was a casual enough manner to disguise the fact that she was very keen to know.

'Could be. Why? Are you trying to tell me that it shows?'

'Something does, but I'm not sure what.'

'Let's just say that I have had my ups and downs and leave it at that,' he said drily. 'The less folk know about me, the less they have to talk about.'

'Huh!' she said scornfully. 'No one knows much about *me*...but you've all been having a field-day!'

She was aware of his bright glance slanting across at her as she went on, 'All *you* should be concerned about, and the same applies to the rest of the staff, is how I function here at Lizzie's. It will be time to start picking at me when I fail on that count. As for the rest of my life— that's my own business.'

'You're not exactly shaking in your shoes at being in

my presence, are you?' he questioned with a grim smile.
'When the boy wonder first started I thought he was going
to start touching his forelock every time I appeared, but
no such deference from you.'

'Why? Is that what you want?' she questioned innocently. 'Yesterday you informed me that you don't stand
on ceremony. That you prefer to be on first-name terms
with the staff—and you *are* based in less than prestigious
hospital accommodation.'

Claudia saw a glitter of anger in the dark eyes that were
looking into hers and knew she was asking for trouble.
The cool flippancy she was adopting was getting to him,
but he gave no sign of it. Instead he answered her in a
similar manner.

'No. It isn't. I don't want you bowing and scraping to
me, but neither do I like your attitude. If you are going to
be accepted by myself and the rest of the staff on
Orthopaedics you need to be more approachable.'

'I *am* approachable—or at least I was, until I found that
the judge and jury had been passing sentence on me during
my absence. That discovery has made me a trifle wary, to
say the least.'

'I can see that I'm wasting my time where you're concerned,' he said flatly. 'You're obviously not in the habit
of listening to reason.'

'Reason! Show it to me—and I'll listen. So far it's been
in very short supply.'

He had a tie on today and a crisp white shirt and she
saw that he was loosening the collar of it as if it were
choking him.

Maybe that was the effect she had on him. Her cheek
had him gasping for breath! But breathless though she
might wish him to be, it hadn't affected his vocal cords.
She couldn't imagine anything ever would.

'Young Holly is safely bedded,' he pronounced, getting back to basics, 'so let's have a look at our latest patient. You know that I operated on her during the night?'

There was no flippancy in her now, just a reluctant respect. 'Yes. I heard,' she said quietly. 'I suppose that's when living on the job comes in handy.'

'Yes. It does. It's convenient at weekends too. I usually work either Saturday or Sunday. The government is forever badgering us to reduce waiting lists—with very good cause, of course.'

'Yes. But it doesn't leave you much time for other things, does it?'

The face that was already one that she wasn't going to forget in a hurry closed up. 'Such as?'

'Family and friends.'

'I'm blessed with an abundance of one—and a shortage of the other.'

Surely he wasn't married...with a house full of little Morrisons? Claudia thought. It would have to be a strong-minded woman who took on this one.

And friends? He was abrupt, bossy, possessed a short fuse if something didn't please him, like a certain red Boxter that had appeared in his sights at the wrong moment. So if he wasn't the life and soul of any party he'd only himself to blame.

Holly's mother was holding her daughter's hand and her father was gently stroking the child's forehead when they stopped by her bed. Their earlier hysterical anger had gone and, emotionally as well as physically exhausted, after a traumatic night, they were anxious to hear what the man who'd fixed their daughter's broken bones had to say.

The little girl was whimpering softly and Lucas spoke to her first, telling her what had happened to her, what he had done to make her better, and that she was going to be in Lizzie's for a little while.

'This is Dr Craven,' he said, glancing over his shoulder to where Claudia was eyeing her sympathetically. 'She and Dr Crawshaw, who is somewhere around, will be here when I'm not and between the three of us we're going to make you better.

'We have lots of games and other interesting things for you to do here and once you've got used to us, Holly, I'm sure you won't mind being in St Elizabeth's one bit.'

To her parents he said in a low voice, 'I explained the extent of Holly's injuries to you shortly after she came out of theatre so I won't go over it all again. The ankle fracture is the most serious, but the fractures of the arms are going to cause the most inconvenience with both of them being in plaster.

'She will have to be fed, washed, taken to the toilet. I'm going to keep her in for a few days and then we'll see. All right?'

Now just as mute as they'd previously been eloquent, her parents nodded and the two doctors moved away.

At that moment Lucas Morrison was called to the phone and as he listened Claudia watched his face tighten.

'When did this happen?' he asked with terse authority and, as the reply came from the other end, went on, 'All right. Don't panic, Sophie. Just look after the baby and I'll be there as quickly as I can.'

So he *was* a family man, Claudia thought as he turned swiftly and said, 'If anyone wants me, I've been called away. I'll be back shortly,' and with the brisk stride that she was beginning to associate with him, he went.

'Where has the "mighty one" gone in such a hurry?' Robin Crawshaw asked when he came in from the next ward.

'Some domestic problem, I think,' Claudia told him as her curiosity about the orthopaedic consultant's private life increased.

'Seems to get a lot of hassle from his family,' he said with a grin, 'and guess what?'

'What?'

'He never gets annoyed with *them*. Well, not often, anyway. Old Morrison takes it out on us instead.'

'He's not old!' Claudia hooted. 'Lucas Morrison is one of the youngest consultants I've come across. I would think that he's a few years to go before he reaches forty, and if his family gives him grief it's probably because he's such a difficult person to get on with.'

She was smiling as she went for a quick coffee before starting on ward rounds. An ally had appeared. It seemed that Robin wasn't prepared to join the Morrison fan club either.

It was the early afternoon before he appeared again and whatever it was that had called him away hadn't sweetened him any.

There was a look of simmering annoyance about him that boded ill for those he was not pleased with—like herself—but to her surprise, when they came face to face outside Dunwoody in the main entrance, he said without rancour, 'You look like a woman with no ties, Claudia Craven. Take my advice and keep it that way.'

'Why, what's wrong?' she asked. 'Family problems? I presume it was your wife on the phone.'

He was staring at her, the wind taken out of his sails for once. 'No way! I'm not married. The call was from my young sister who is so used to my being there for her that she calls me if her little finger hurts, as does my brother who is playing at being a student.

'Although on this occasion Sophie *did* have a problem

in the form of an estranged husband demanding to see his child and threatening violence if he didn't.'

'And so what did you do?'

He ran his hands through dark waves cut short upon his head and said matter of factly, 'Told him to apply through the proper channels, then sent him packing.'

'And will she be safe now?' Claudia asked, with visions of the irate father returning.

'Sophie is in my flat at the moment, which is going to be a tight squash with the two of us and baby Craig. But at least I've got her where I can make sure she comes to no harm.'

'It's clear that you don't get much time to do your own thing,' she commented.

'My "own thing", as you describe it, is what I do here,' he said brusquely. 'I wanted to be a doctor from the day that I discovered we couldn't afford to pay for our prescriptions when we were ill. A situation that I'm sure *you* have never found yourself in.

'I was eleven at the time and tired of the poverty that had been thrust upon us after my father walked out. I had a desire to be on the other side of the fence—amongst those who dished out the care, instead of wishing they could afford it.'

'You are much to be admired,' Claudia found herself saying with stilted sincerity. He certainly was, but why tell *her* all this? It was only yesterday that he'd said the less that was known about him, the better. Yet here he was, painting a picture of dependent relatives...and the grimly determined ability that had got him where he was. They must have broken the mould after this man had been fashioned.

But the revelation of life according to Lucas Morrison

was over. 'What's been happening in my absence?' he
wanted to know. 'Any problems?'

Claudia shook her head. 'Not to my knowledge. Is it
today that you're going to decide whether to splint the
baby with the hip deformity?'

One of his rare smiles flashed out and she thought how
different he looked when he wasn't frowning. There was
a hawkish sort of attractiveness about him that some
women would find mesmerising, but not her.

The memory of a thin, tanned face with a quirky smile
and sad blue eyes was the one that pulled at *her* heart-
strings. And that was how it was always going to be—just
a memory of a time she would never forget.

He was answering her question and eyeing her keenly
at the same time as if aware that her mind was in some
far place.

'Yes. I am going to decide what to do with that particular child...amongst others,' he was saying, but the thing
that Claudia had been dreading was happening. The sounds
of that last day were crowding in on her again—the babble
of the flea market, the gentle lapping of the waves beneath
the golden sun—and she felt herself slipping into some
sort of hazy other world, unaware that she was calling
Jack's name.

But reality was creeping back. She could hear a voice
urgently calling *her* name. Someone's arms were holding
her close and as she sagged against a hard chest the moment passed.

'What in God's name is the matter?' Lucas Morrison
was asking as she opened her eyes. 'Are you ill?'

Claudia shook her head. 'Not in the true sense. The
memory of something that happened to me some months
ago comes back sometimes and takes over my mind.'

'I see,' he said slowly. 'And who is Jack?'

She turned her head away, easing herself out of his arms at the same time. 'Just a friend,' she said quietly. 'I'm sorry to have involved you.'

He was back to his abrupt self. 'Don't mention it. Are you well enough to carry on, or would you like to go home?'

'No, of course not,' she said immediately. 'It was just a memory from the past that caught me off guard.'

'And you're not going to tell me what it was that put you in such a state?'

'No, I'm not. You aren't the only one who likes to keep their affairs to themselves, and now, if you'll excuse me, I'll get back to the ward.'

'Yes, of course. Never let it be said that I kept you away from those whom we strive to make into "straight" children.'

Lucas watched her walk away from him, a slender, erect figure, with a plait of golden hair that swung gently as she moved. He shook his head. The newest member of his team was a cool customer. Almost hard, in fact. Probably a woman who wouldn't be easily intimidated...and yet only seconds ago she'd slumped into his arms in a state of complete vulnerability and he wanted to know why.

'I see that you've got young Dr Craven back with you on Orthopaedics,' Mrs Lewis said from behind the counter of Dunwoody when he went in to buy the flowers that had been the reason for him being in that part of the hospital.

'Er, yes. Do you know her?' he questioned.

'I used to before she went off like she did. Doesn't seem the same girl since she came back. I saw her in the staff restaurant yesterday, but she wasn't ready for a chat like she would have been at one time.'

Lucas was standing with the flowers in his arms, won-

dering if the shopkeeper was going to vouch any more
information about his new member of staff. It appeared
that she was and he was amazed just how much he wanted
to hear it.

'Her father is Charles Craven, the property tycoon. They
have a large house in one of the Cotswold villages and a
villa in Italy,' Mrs Lewis informed him. 'Claudia never
used to talk about it much but you could tell that she'd
been brought up in the lap of luxury.'

He turned away. This was the last thing he wanted to
hear. All he was interested in hearing about Claudia
Craven was if she was up to the job. Nothing else mattered.

'Fancy coming for a coffee?' Robin Crawshaw asked as
they went off duty at three in the afternoon.

Claudia hesitated. She'd been up at half-past five to get
to Lizzie's in time for the early shift's seven o'clock start,
and wanted to call in at one of the stores before she drove
home.

But she'd enjoyed making the young doctor's acquaintance. He was uncomplicated and easy to be with. She
knew instinctively they were going to be friends, so why
not celebrate their future working relationship with a quick
coffee?

'I'd love to,' she told him

Apart from the fact that she'd taken an instant liking to
him, she had few enough friends here at Lizzie's, so every
one counted.

As they left the big grey building together, leaving their
cars behind as they made for a small bistro a hundred yards
away, Claudia saw Lucas Morrison striding in the direction
of the staff quarters.

Robin had seen him too and he remarked with droll
deference, 'There is he to whom we bow the knee.'

'Rubbish!' she hooted laughingly. 'He doesn't like that sort of thing.'

'Not from a classy bird like you, maybe, but he likes to keep *me* on my toes.'

'He doesn't see me as anything but a cog on the wheel,' she protested, 'and in any case Lucas Morrison is very much aware of the difference in our backgrounds.'

'You mean because *you're* rich and *he's* poor?'

'*Was*, maybe, but I wouldn't think that applies now, not from what we know about consultants' pay.'

She was thinking that maybe for once he was finishing early, or perhaps he was going to check on mother and child, but she wasn't going to mention either surmise to Robin. Especially the latter as she didn't know what the hospital rules were with regard to staff having outsiders living with them in the small flatlets.

Although, knowing the man, it wouldn't bother him if it *wasn't* allowed. She had a very strong feeling that treading on the toes of others didn't worry him unduly.

Yet it seemed that his natural arrogance wasn't always to the fore. He'd lumbered himself with another man's child, albeit temporarily, and seemed willing to be there for his brother and sister when they needed him, which made her think that his parents weren't alive.

That would be something else that *she* had and *he* hadn't. Hers were the best parents in the world. They had watched her grieve over Jack with loving anguish, doing all they could to lessen the pain. But only time, or love for someone else, could do that and she thought perhaps the man hadn't been born who could make her as happy as Jack had.

But why all these comparisons and heart-searchings? she asked herself as they seated themselves at an empty table in the bistro. You haven't known Lucas Morrison for five minutes. The only link between you is Lizzie's. So why keep dwelling on the man and his mannerisms?

As they chatted over their coffee Claudia discovered that Robin Crawshaw came from a medical family. Both his parents were GPs and his older sister a nurse at another London hospital.

'It gets a bit claustrophobic at times,' he said with his ready smile. 'I wonder sometimes if I should have gone into the building trade. I've always been fascinated by cement mixers.'

'You *are* in the building trade,' she told him laughingly. 'Rebuilding, anyway. Putting the bones and bodies of young ones together again. That's what orthopaedics is all about. What could be more rewarding?'

'You sound like Lucas. He sees it like that.'

'Well, he would, wouldn't he? He hasn't got to where he is at his age without a lot of hard work and dedication,' she reasoned, 'but we haven't come in here to talk about *him*. What sort of a social life does your job at Lizzie's allow?'

He groaned dramatically. 'None. I shall probably end up well and truly on the shelf.'

'That makes two of us, then.'

'Not *you*, surely?' he expostulated. 'I'm surprised that you aren't already in a relationship.'

'I was, but it's over,' she said quietly.

'What happened?'

'I'd rather not talk about it, if you don't mind, Robin.'

'Sure,' he said easily and there was something in his tone that made her wonder if he was happy to know that she was unattached. She hoped not.

* * *

Her mother rang in the early evening and as soon as she heard her voice Claudia curled up on the couch next to the phone and prepared for a lengthy chat.

'How is it going at Lizzie's?' were Helen Craven's first words.

'Fine, Mum,' she fibbed.

There was no way that Claudia was going to inform her parents that most of the staff on the orthopaedic unit were antagonistic or that the man who would have the biggest effect on her working life there was autocratic and soon irritated.

They were concerned enough about her as it was, and if they had the slightest inkling that she wasn't happy to be back at St Elizabeth's they would be even more worried.

Jack's parents lived near to her own and the four of them had consoled each other since his death, while at the same time showing in every way possible how sorry they were for its tragic effect upon herself.

'So you feel that going back there was the right decision?' her mother asked, not entirely convinced.

Claudia didn't need to lie this time. Whatever she might have to put up with from those she worked with, it hadn't made her change her mind. She might not have their approval, but it didn't stop her from admiring the excellent nursing they provided for the sick children in their care.

And, in any case, going back to Lizzie's was helping to fill the aching void that her life had become and nothing—no one—was going to deprive her of that.

So she replied, 'Yes. Definitely. I've no regrets.' Then with a quick change of subject, 'How's Dad?'

'Missing you,' her mother said gently, 'and he wants to know how the Boxter is running.'

That was soon answered. 'Smooth as silk.'

She wasn't going to tell her mother that it had been the cause of her starting off on the wrong foot at Lizzie's.

'And so is Anthony Bellingham still the top man in the orthopaedic section?' was the next question coming her way.

Claudia wriggled uncomfortably against the cushions of the couch. Why couldn't they talk about the weather?

'No. He's retired.'

'And who's taken his place?'

'A much younger, high-flyer type.'

'Is that so? Sounds interesting.'

'Not really. He's the personification of the three "A"'s. Abrupt, abrasive, and arrogant.'

'Oh!' her mother exclaimed. 'What a daunting combination. Obviously, you're not impressed.'

That was not the case. She was impressed, all right. She hadn't christened him the urban tiger for nothing, and there wasn't a more impressive animal to be found than the tiger.

Later, as she lay in the winter darkness, Claudia's mind switched to the moments when Lucas Morrison had held her in that strong, safe embrace.

It had been her first physical contact with any member of the opposite sex since Jack's death. How different it had been from *his* final weak embraces.

There had been power and purpose in the arms that had held her in the corridor outside Dunwoody. She'd been aware of it, in spite of the state she'd been in.

For a strange, unsettling fraction of time, and at the least likely moment, she'd felt comforted—by him of all people! Even though she knew that the only emotion it had aroused in *him* was curiosity.

CHAPTER THREE

FEBRUARY had given way to the cold winds of March and as each day of the English winter came and went the shimmering heat of India seemed a little farther away.

Claudia was finding that the work on the wards and in the clinics was enough to send her home at the end of each day too tired to brood, and if there *was* still a lack of acceptance by some of the staff, her friendship with Robin Crawshaw made up for it.

Although she sensed that he was attracted to her, the likeable young doctor had made no attempt to be anything other than friendly, as if he sensed that any other approach would not be welcome, and she was grateful for his thoughtfulness.

Sometimes when they were chatting together in the staff room, or sharing a table in the restaurant, she would be aware of the penetrating gaze of Lucas Morrison and find herself holding her breath as if she'd been caught out doing something wrong.

She had enquired about his sister's welfare a couple of times since the day he'd brought her and her child to his flat, and been told that there had been a truce between the warring couple. That for the time being all was well.

Her second enquiry had been a couple of days ago and he'd said drily, 'The state of bliss continues for the moment and as my contribution to its survival I'm having the baby for the weekend to give them some time alone.'

Claudia had gaped at him and, tuning into her thoughts,

he'd said, 'I presume that look of doubtful amazement is because you can't see me pushing a pram?'

'Er...something like that,' she'd admitted.

'Well, let's just say I won't be needing an L-plate. I've pushed the child's mother and our younger brother out many a time in the past.'

His words had conjured up a vision of a scrawny young lad, with dark hair and eyes and a strong sense of responsibility, pushing a battered old pram with two young tots in it, and she'd wondered if he was winding her up, deliberately placing more emphasis on the difference between them.

He'd read her thoughts again. 'It's true, Claudia. There are things I've had to do that you, with your pampered lifestyle, haven't heard of.'

She'd believed him, but wished he wouldn't keep bringing the subject up. It was almost as if he was using their different backgrounds as a safety-valve.

And now it was the Saturday afternoon of the weekend Lucas was babysitting. Claudia had been working on the early shift again and Robin was on a couple of days' leave, so she was alone as she came out of the hospital.

It was a cold, blustery day and, with her coat wrapped tightly around her and head bent against the wind, she was about to descend to where the Boxter was parked.

When she looked up Lucas was strolling towards her pushing a high coach-built pram. He was dressed for the weather in a black suede jacket, above a thick white sweater and jeans, and for once he wasn't moving with his usual urgency.

Caught up in the surprise of the moment, Claudia said the first thing that came into her head. 'What a lovely pram! How much better than all the canvas folding efforts that look as if a gust of wind would blow them away.'

Dark brows lifted ironically as he told her, 'It was *my* choice. I'll bet *you* had one of these when you were an infant. A Silver Cross, or suchlike.'

Claudia sighed. He was doing it again.

'I've no idea what I was pushed around in. I don't suppose it was a wooden buggy on wheels, but does it matter?'

She bent over the pram and saw a tiny baby boy lying snugly beneath the covers. 'He's sweet,' she said softly.

'He wasn't at two o'clock this morning.'

'So you've been in charge since yesterday?'

'Yes. Sophie and Dimitri left last night and are due back tomorrow evening.'

'Dimitri?'

'Yes. He's Greek. She used to work in his restaurant until he made her pregnant.'

'And you weren't pleased about that?'

'No. I was not,' he said heavily. 'She's only nineteen...and he's in his early thirties. I keep wondering if he's got another wife tucked away somewhere. But I'll concern myself about that if and when it happens.'

The baby stirred in his sleep and Lucas rocked the pram gently as he asked, 'What's been happening on the unit today? Anything I need to know about? You knew that Miles Soper was on call? He seems to be reasonably well at the moment but how long it will last, I don't know.'

Claudia was only half listening. She wanted to laugh. Firstly at the thought of the chained tiger pacing the bedroom in the early hours with his small nephew, and secondly at the incongruity of the pair of them hovering over the pram like doting parents, when the child inside it belonged to neither of them.

But he'd asked a question and was waiting for an answer and, as the 'babysitter' wasn't renowned for his patience, she brought her mind to bear on present matters.

'No. Nothing out of the ordinary has happened,' she told him. 'No new admissions. No crisis situations…and no improvement in relations between Sheila Newcome and myself.

'The rest of the nursing staff seem to be mellowing now that they realise I'm no different from anyone else, in that I work hard, eat with a knife and fork, and breathe in and out like the rest of them. But that woman is bitter and twisted.'

'She's a lot on her mind at the moment,' he said soberly. 'Sheila has a sick husband, a severely handicapped child in a home, and she was burgled recently.'

Under normal circumstances Claudia would have felt profound sympathy for someone in that kind of situation, but *she* wasn't to blame for any of it. Life hadn't been exactly kind to her of recent months, but she wasn't making someone else pay for it.

'And so she hits out at me?' she said flatly. 'The first person to appear in her sights? I'd say that was hardly fair. But perhaps you agree with her. Maybe she's not the only one who thinks I'm from another planet because we don't dine with the milk bottle on the table.'

His laughter when it came bursting forth was a rare sound. 'Hardly! Even *we* had a jug for the milk when I was a kid…although it did have a crack in it.'

This conversation was getting them nowhere, she decided, and she was beginning to feel cold standing there on the windswept pavement.

'I'm going,' she said. 'I hope that your child-minding goes well.'

'It will,' he said with his usual cool confidence. 'As I've already explained—I've had plenty of practice.'

He was something else! Claudia thought as she drove home. Jack of all trades and master of them all. Had *anything* ever shaken his confidence?

Belinda Brown had asked her round for a meal that evening, and as Claudia dressed for the occasion it felt strange. She hadn't been out socially since before she and Jack had set off on the round-the-world trip.

In a black beaded top, matching velvet trousers, and with silver high-heeled sandals on her feet, she was satisfied with her ensemble, and when she'd brushed the golden swathe of her hair free of its neat plait Claudia looked what she was: a beautiful young woman.

Yet that wasn't how she saw herself. She felt dried up and shrivelled with grief. Losing the man she loved had made her feel older than her years…and forsaken. It was something that she knew she had to fight—the emptiness that came from loss—but it wasn't getting any easier.

The first thing Claudia heard as she stepped over the threshold of the smart mews house where Belinda lived with her husband and teenage sons was the sound of a baby crying and it stopped her in her tracks.

Twice in one day she'd been near a tiny baby. There would have been nothing strange about it on the wards, but outside Lizzie's it was most unusual.

'We've got an extra mouth to feed tonight,' Belinda said as she gave her a welcoming hug, 'but the young man in question has brought his own food: a bottle of breast milk expressed earlier by his mother.'

At the same second as she realised that her friend was referring to the baby that she'd seen in the afternoon outside Lizzie's, she saw Lucas walking around the room at the far end of the hall with a red-faced bundle in his arms.

'Belinda! How could you?' she whispered angrily.

The plump medical secretary laughed. 'I could...and I have. The only thing I didn't bargain for was Lucas Morrison bringing some competition with him.'

'It's as well he did,' Claudia hissed. 'It might take his mind off the fact that he's been set up. For your information he is the last man in the world I would look at...and in any case...'

'All right,' Belinda soothed. 'I admit it was tactless of me, but I can't bear to see you so unhappy.'

'Maybe, but fobbing me off on to the man who rules the roost on Orthopaedics isn't going to cheer me up.'

If she'd any further complaints about her hostess's plotting Claudia didn't get the chance to voice them. Lucas Morrison had seen her and was heading in her direction.

As she braced herself for what was bound to be an uncomfortable second meeting of the day, he amazed her by holding out the crying child and saying, ' Here, take him. Maybe you can calm Craig down,' and without further ado he placed the baby in her arms and picked up a glass of sherry.

He had some nerve, she thought as the baby's cries dwindled away. When they'd met earlier he'd been bragging how good he was with infants, but he'd met his match with this one, and as the baby snuggled up to her soft curves she understood why.

This was a naturally fed child, used to sucking from his mother's breasts. The hard chest of the baby minder must have seemed like a barren land.

'You didn't tell me that you were dining here tonight,' Lucas said as the baby's eyelashes swept down onto its tiny cheeks.

'Why should I? I had no idea that you and baby Craig were invited too.'

'He wasn't. When Belinda asked me to dine with them earlier in the week I didn't know that I was going to be having him for the weekend. My lusty nephew is a gate-crasher.'

'I thought you had a lot of experience with infants?' Claudia questioned innocently. 'Only you didn't seem to be doing too well when I arrived.'

'I *do* have the experience, but didn't allow for not having the right kind of breasts,' he said casually as his eyes rested on the enticing mounds that the baby was nestling against.

When Claudia had seen his sister's baby the first time the little one had been tucked up in the pram, but now the whole of him was visible and as her glance moved down towards his feet she gave a gasp of dismay. They were both inturned from the ankles.

Lucas Morrison had heard the sound and didn't need to question its cause. 'Talipes...club-foot,' he said briefly. 'Massaging has had no effect, so I'm going to try plaster casts for a few months. If that doesn't work I will have him admitted to Lizzie's. It will be the first time I've operated on one of my own.'

'You never mentioned it this afternoon,' she commented.

'Why should I? You're not entitled to a running commentary of what's going on in my life.'

So now it was his turn to be flip, though she could sense the concern in him. But no child could be in better hands than those of this unpredictable bone-straightener. When she got back to her apartment she would read up everything she could find about the deformity.

'Know anything about it?' he was asking with his usual sparsity of speech.

'A bit,' she admitted warily, praying that he wasn't going to start firing questions at her in Belinda's house of all places.

'I know that the problem is more common in boys than girls,' she said carefully. 'And in an older child it can be connected with a neurological disorder such as spina bifida, cerebral palsy, or polio.'

He nodded. 'Correct, so far, and…?'

'We're ready to eat, folks,' Belinda called from the kitchen and she was saved.

With the exception of the sleeping child they were the only guests of the Brown family and Claudia prayed that, if Lucas was aware of his hostess's scheming, he wouldn't think that she had anything to do with it. It would be totally embarrassing if he did.

The last thing she wanted at this time in her life was to be involved with another man. She was too upset and vulnerable and, if ever she did want another relationship, it wouldn't be with *this* man who was a control freak.

But with that thought came another. He might be the 'big controller' but he'd done one thing for her: he'd made her feel alive again. She'd thrown off some of the apathy that had overwhelmed her. Maybe a gradual healing process was about to begin.

But did she want that to happen? If she stopped grieving for Jack it would be disloyal to his memory…as if he had never been part of her life.

Light-hearted chatter was going on around her and as Claudia tuned back into the moment Belinda's husband, Bernard, an amiable college lecturer, was saying, 'This is very pleasant, having you both dining with us. We must do it again.'

'No!' Claudia cried before she could stop herself.

As she looked around her in the silence that followed her involuntary protest, she saw that Belinda was staring down fixedly at her plate. That her husband's smile had become a puzzled grimace. That the boys were exchanging amused glances—and the man who was the reason for her sudden outburst was observing her with a glance as cold as the night outside.

'Er—all my spare time is going to be tied up in the near future, I'm afraid,' she stammered untruthfully as her colour rose in a warm, embarrassed tide. 'But it's ever so nice to be invited into your home, Bernard. Maybe when I'm less pressured you and Belinda will dine with *me*?'

If Lucas Morrison's glance had been cold before, it was glacial now. He couldn't help but be aware that he hadn't been included in the half-hearted invitation.

And so what? Belinda had got her here under false pretences. The sooner she nipped it all in the bud, the better.

But it wasn't going to be that easy. She might have known that the 'urban tiger' wouldn't let her get away with it, without having some comment to make.

It came within minutes of them leaving the Brown residence together. Claudia had tried to hang on, giving him the chance to depart before she left, but Lucas wasn't having any of that.

The baby was still asleep in his carry-cot so there was no urgency for him to leave on that score, and, short of asking the Browns for a bed for the night, she had to face the fact that whether she liked it or not they were going to be departing at the same time.

'At least you've made one thing clear,' he said coolly as they walked towards their cars, he carrying the baby, she with her face huddled in the collar of her coat.

'What's that?' she mumbled.

'That you had no part in tonight's cosy little get-together…that you would rather have been anywhere than with me.'

'You soon catch on, don't you?' she flipped back uncomfortably.

'Maybe not as quickly as you think, but, after the way you almost freaked out at the thought of another evening in my company, I'm not going to have any doubts about where I stand with you in the future. What is it with you?' he growled. 'You're like some prickly virgin who's afraid of the big bad wolf.'

Claudia began to laugh, knowing that if she didn't she would start howling like an infant—and there was already one of those present. 'My virginity is not up for discussion, and I don't see *you* as a big bad wolf.'

He sighed. 'Well, I suppose that's something. What *do* you see me as?'

'A force to be reckoned with?'

That brought a smile to break up the severity of his face. 'I really did start on the wrong foot with you, didn't I?' he said. 'I admit I was crabby that morning—with good reason, but I shouldn't have griped about your car the way I did.

'I'd just had Sophie on the phone full of her self-inflicted troubles, to be followed almost immediately by my young brother's landlady asking for his overdue rent. The young scallywag had assured me that he was managing financially, when all the time he wasn't. So what with one thing and another…'

They had reached her car and as Claudia fished in her pocket for the keys she was trying to choose the right words to make him understand why she was wary of him, without telling him the full truth.

Whatever else he was, here was a man who didn't shirk

his responsibilities. A man of taciturn integrity, who didn't beat about the bush in his dealings with others.

If he did have feelings, she'd just trampled on them back there at the Browns' house. Yet why shouldn't she make it clear that she didn't crave his company? She was a free agent…now.

'You don't need to apologise about that time in the lift,' she told him. 'We all say things when we're under pressure that we afterwards regret. If I come over as wary when I'm in your company, it's partly because you can be very intimidating at times. But there's another reason why I prefer to keep myself to myself.'

'And that is?'

'Let's just say that while I was on that trip around the world something awful happened to me.'

His face showed shock. 'God! You were raped?'

Claudia shook her head. 'No. Not anything like that.'

'The fellow you were with ditched you?'

'He left me…yes.'

'How well did you know him?'

'As well as I know myself.'

'So you're a bad judge of character.'

'Maybe I am,' she said bleakly.

He was making her sound like some easily led bimbo and she couldn't go on…couldn't get the words out to make him understand.

Leaning against the side of the car, she put her head into her hands, praying that the torturous memories wouldn't come crowding back to complicate matters further.

He was placing the carry-cot with its precious occupant carefully onto the bonnet of the car, and when he was satisfied that it was safe he put his hand beneath her chin and lifted her face to meet his.

'You're a fool if you're still moping after someone who

deserted you like that,' he said harshly. 'You treat *me* as if I've got the plague, and I haven't done anything!'

'He had no choice,' she told him in a voice so low he had to bend his head to hear the words. 'The trip was Jack's dying wish. He had terminal fibrosarcoma. He refused a leg amputation and radiotherapy when he was told that the cancer was very advanced and that treatment would only give a brief respite, and set his heart on one last fling.

'Jack died on a remote beach in India. I can still see the blood from the massive haemorrhage that was the actual cause of his death staining the sand…and there was nothing I could do.'

If she'd expected him to show compassion or horror at her tragic loss it wasn't immediately forthcoming. 'You could have kept him within reach of medical help,' he said quietly. 'Instead of wandering off the beaten track.'

'Don't you think that was what I wanted?' she cried. 'It was his wishes that mattered. It's typical of *you* to take that attitude. Always practicalities! No room for emotion! You're the nearest thing to a robot I've ever come across!'

There was a light in his eyes that she hadn't seen before. 'Is that so?' he questioned smoothly.

He took her hand and pressed it against his cheek. 'Does that feel like tin?' Before she could reply he was unbuttoning his jacket and putting her palm on his chest where she could feel the strong beat of his heart. 'And is that some sort of mechanism that you hear?'

'No. It isn't,' she said weakly.

He nodded as if satisfied to have proved his point. 'So, if I seem cold and unfeeling it's because I've never had the time to develop relationships. They've always seemed too time-consuming. But I have to admit that I've never seen myself as repulsive as you seem to find me.'

'I don't,' she protested, and was amazed to find that she meant it. Whether it was because she'd brought her grief over Jack out into the open, or whether after today's happenings she was beginning to see him in a new light, she didn't know. But one thing she did know was that Lucas Morrison's nearness was affecting her.

Claudia could smell his aftershave, see the tired lines around the observant dark eyes, and the even white teeth that were biting into his bottom lip. A gesture that in anyone else she might have put down to indecision, but not him. She couldn't imagine him ever having been hesitant about anything in his life.

And he wasn't hesitating now. He was taking the hand that still lay upon his chest into his, and his other arm was drawing her towards him.

'You're too young and beautiful to be living in the past, Claudia Craven,' he said with his eyes on her lips, 'no matter how much you loved this Jack of yours. And with regard to myself, maybe it's time that I got some practice in, as you find me to be so lacking in empathy.'

'No!' she protested as panic swept over her, but he chose not to listen and as his mouth came down on hers, gently at first and then with a fierce arousal that made her cling to him in traitorous response, the past seemed far, far away, and the present all that mattered.

How long it was before she came to her senses, Claudia didn't know. They were both hungry for each other and loth to admit they'd had their fill, but she drew away at last as reason asserted itself.

As he looked down on her, his face in shadow from the street lamps, Lucas showed that he read her thoughts once again.

'You're thinking that you've been disloyal to his memory, aren't you?' he said flatly. 'And with *me* of all people.'

She nodded miserably. 'Yes. Something like that.'

'Then there's nothing more to be said, is there?' Picking up the carry-cot that held his still-sleeping nephew, he went striding down the road with the brisk grace that was so much a part of him, to where his own car was parked.

It took all of Sunday for Claudia to recover from Saturday night's 'fever' and all the time the main thought in her mind was that she should have seen it coming, should have realised that her awareness of everything Lucas said or did had to mean something.

Her panic when Belinda's husband had suggested another get-together hadn't been because she disliked Lucas, but because he affected her as no man ever had, and if she was being disloyal to gentle Jack there was nothing she could do about it.

But the thought of another relationship terrified her. If she gave in to the longing that he had aroused in her, she would be achingly vulnerable again, and, knowing the kind of man he was, she couldn't stand the thought of any more pain.

By Monday morning she was feeling less fraught and she presented herself on the wards with a calm that came from a decision to act as if nothing had happened.

Sheila Newcome was her usual sour self and for once the nurse's acerbity wasn't unwelcome, as it brought the touch of normality to the day that Claudia needed.

When Lucas came striding onto the ward she was having a discussion with Jess Richardson about the condition of a small girl who had been admitted late on Saturday and had been seen by the consultant on call, Miles Soper.

'Mr Soper left a message to say that he'd thought it

better to leave Olivia's treatment until Lucas came in this morning,' Jess was explaining, 'as he was going away on holiday first thing yesterday and didn't want to get involved.'

I'll bet, Claudia thought angrily. That man is never here. I wonder how long it is since Lucas had a holiday.

She shook her head in self-chiding. You are not supposed to be getting involved with *anything* regarding Lucas Morrison, she told herself as the man who had opened the floodgates of longing the previous night converged on them.

'So what's with this one, Sister?' he asked with a brief nod in Claudia's direction.

'Admitted late Saturday, Lucas,' she replied, 'with a left-sided limp and pains in the same leg. She'd had the problem for a few days and her parents eventually brought her into Accident and Emergency. Mr Soper saw her and has left her to you, as he's now on vacation. There have been no recent infections of any kind or previous hip problems, but the movements in that area are limited.

'So we'll have a look at Olivia, shall we, Dr Craven?' he said crisply. 'And we'll have your comments first.'

She'd been expecting this and thought, Please don't freeze up on me, Lucas, or try to catch me out. Can't we go back to how we were before Saturday?

'There *are* only limited hip movements, but I don't detect any other joint involvement,' she told him after a careful examination, during which he'd observed her without expression.

'So what do you suggest we do?' he asked blandly, after he'd examined the child himself.

'Full blood count, throat swab, and hip X-rays?' she said carefully.

'So let's get them done, shall we?' he said, and left her
to it.

'So what's with the "whiz-kid" this morning?' Robin
asked as they sat together in the restaurant at lunch-time.
'He's like a bear with a sore head.'

'Or a tiger that's miffed,' she murmured.

'Wha-at?'

Claudia smiled. 'Don't mind me. I was just thinking out
loud.'

'How did it go at the Browns' on Saturday night?' was
his next question, as if he sensed a connection.

'Er...interesting. Lucas was there.'

'So how did you get on?'

'Better than I would have expected,' she told him breez-
ily. After all, they *had* kissed, but she wasn't going to
mention that!

'So he's less overpowering when he's away from
Lizzie's, then?'

'I suppose so.'

She didn't suppose anything of the kind. She knew he
wasn't. His impact had been mind-blowing to say the least
if those moments under the street lamp with baby Craig
sleeping peacefully beside them were anything to go by.

At that moment he came into the restaurant with a tall,
willowy brunette at his side and Claudia felt herself tens-
ing. There was something in the manner of the two of them
that spoke of easy intimacy and she found herself wondering uneasily who the new face might belong to.

'Who's that with Lucas?' she asked casually of Robin,
who was more interested in his meal than the comings and
goings of others.

'She works in the social services office here,' he said
with little interest.

'What's she called?' Claudia persisted.

'Marina Beauchamp.'

'I haven't seen her before.'

'You'll have had no cause to, will you?'

'No. I suppose not.' There was silence for a moment and then she went on, 'They seem to be on very good terms.'

'Who? Morrison and Beauchamp? Why so interested? I thought you couldn't stand him.'

'That's putting words into my mouth,' she protested.

He was about to embark on the sweet course and was giving more attention to the piece of lemon meringue pie in front of him than the behaviour of the orthopaedic consultant.

As Lucas and his companion seated themselves at a table nearby Claudia was able to observe Marina Beauchamp and seeing her more closely made her feel even more edgy.

Extremely attractive in a flashy sort of way, Marina had long dark hair, a liberal application of make-up on her olive skin, and a figure that a lot of women would die for.

She was holding forth on some subject or other and Lucas was totally engrossed in what she was saying, nodding in agreement every so often.

He looked up suddenly and caught Claudia watching them, and as her colour deepened he gave a casual wave in their direction.

But Marina didn't even stop for breath and as he went back to giving her his full attention Claudia was surprised to find how irritated she was at the picture of complete absorption in each other that they presented.

So he wasn't the intimidator with everybody, she thought sombrely. But she knew that already, didn't she? She'd seen him with the children on the wards and with his young nephew, and from all accounts he was a soft touch when it came to his brother and sister.

Yet *that* sort of protectiveness could stem from the fact that their parents were dead and Lucas, being the eldest, had set himself up in their place.

He'd said the previous night that relationships of any other kind were too time-consuming...so what category did this intense meeting come under? One thing was for sure, they weren't discussing the weather.

CHAPTER FOUR

DURING the week that followed there were two interesting happenings on the orthopaedic unit at St Elizabeth's.

The first was the arrival on Outpatients of a pretty auburn-haired girl and a swarthy older man who was carrying the baby that Claudia had last seen in his carry-cot on the bonnet of her car.

She was assisting Lucas that morning and when they appeared he said in brief introduction, 'My sister, Sophie, and her husband, Dimitri. The third member of the party you already know,' and to the oddly matched parents, 'Meet Dr Claudia Craven who is already aware of Craig's problem.'

'There should not be a problem!' the baby's father said angrily. 'The cheeldren of my family haf always been strong. It ees this cold country that has done thees to my son.'

'Your son *is* strong, Dimitri,' Lucas said decisively, 'and healthy. The club-foot is a birth defect, probably caused by his mother's uterus pressing on his feet during pregnancy.

'There are various ways to deal with the deformity. We always try manipulation and massage first, and if that is not successful, as in Craig's case, the next thing is a plaster cast on each leg. That is why you're here today, so that I can supervise it being done exactly as I want it.'

The Greek nodded morosely, satisfied that his honour was intact in the knowledge that his wife was supposedly to blame for the club-foot.

'So you see, Dimmy, you aren't any less of a man than you thought you were,' the copper-haired Sophie teased. 'It's the fault of the narrow-hipped English girl that you got pregnant.'

'Stop it, Sophie,' Lucas ordered. 'There are more important things to be discussed here than who's to blame for what, such as your son's future mobility.'

'Any comments?' he asked when they'd gone, with the baby protesting lustily at the restriction of his legs.

'What about?' Claudia asked warily, not sure if he was referring to his nephew's treatment or the child's parents.

'Sophie...and Dimitri.'

'Your sister's very pretty,' she said slowly, 'and her husband seems typical of his race. Proud, family-minded...and small.'

She was looking up at the lithe, upright figure beside her and knew that in comparison to this man all the rest of his sex would seem less in stature.

Not because he was a giant, but because there was something about Lucas Morrison that was commanding. She'd thought at first that it was his ego, but she was having to think again about that.

If he was brusque at times it was because he'd been brought up in a hard school. If he seemed arrogant it was the perfectionist in him revealing itself, and if he wanted those under him, like Robin and herself, to eventually become as efficient as he, the man was entitled to 'keep them on their toes' as the young doctor had described it.

'Dimitri may not be tall, I agree,' Lucas was saying, 'but the man doesn't see himself as anything less than magnificent...and I'm afraid that my crazy young sister sees him in the same light.'

'Then you have nothing to worry about. If they are

equally devoted,' Claudia commented absently as she
brought her thoughts into line. What was the matter with
her? She'd just been making excuses for Lucas Morrison—
praising him, even! If she wasn't careful the small Dimitri
wouldn't be the only one with a woman who doted on
him.

But maybe Lucas already had someone who'd set her
sights on him. What about Marina, the dark-haired beauty
who'd had him so engrossed that day in the restaurant?

The second interesting happening on the orthopaedic
wards was the admission of a teenage boy, who surprisingly was accompanied by Marina.

In keeping with the rapport that had been obvious on
that other occasion, Lucas made a point of being there to
greet them as they came into the ward and to Claudia it
meant that they must be of special importance if the orthopaedic consultant was waiting for them.

'Marina,' he said with brisk pleasantness as she and the
boy walked along the polished floor towards him, 'and
Peter,' with a reassuring smile for the lad who looked miserable and embarrassed.

To Jess Richardson and herself who were hovering curiously he said, 'This young man is Peter Beauchamp. I
saw him at home the other day and have brought him in
for tests. Peter has a swollen and painful upper arm and
we're going to find out what's causing it.'

'If you'd like to take over, Jess, and get him settled in,
Dr Craven and I will have a chat with his mother in my
office,' he told the ward sister and, with a curt nod for
Claudia to follow them, he led the way, with the dark-
haired Marina by his side.

As Claudia trailed along behind them she was trying to
work out what it was all about. Lucas didn't have private

patients. So that wasn't the reason why this woman and her son were being given the VIP treatment.

And in any case, if he had been intending to treat the boy privately they wouldn't be here. He would have him admitted to one of the many private hospitals dotted around London.

Which left only one conclusion. He and Marina Beauchamp must be on very close terms, and as a vision of what those 'terms' might be presented itself she was amazed to find that she was uneasy.

She could tell that he sensed her curiosity and, after he'd asked Marina to be seated and Claudia had gone to stand by the window with her hands deep in the pockets of her white hospital coat, he said, 'Marina is very worried about Peter. He's all she's got. His father, who was a friend of mine, was killed in Ulster.'

Claudia felt herself relaxing. So *that* was the connection. Or was it? It could still be a case of the widow and the whiz-kid.

'I'm going to send Peter for X-rays and a bone biopsy,' he was telling Marina. 'When I get the results from them I'll have a better idea of what the problem is and we'll take it from there.'

She got to her feet. 'Tell me that you don't think it's serious,' she pleaded.

'I can't,' he said sombrely. 'It wouldn't be fair, Marina. What I *can* tell you is that if it *is* anything to worry about I will do everything in my power to put it right.'

'Yes. I know you will,' she said trustingly. 'And now I must go to Peter as he was very loth to come here today.'

When she'd gone Claudia asked, 'How old is the boy?'

'Thirteen,' he said, 'and I have a bad feeling about this one. Marina had taken him to their GP who didn't seem to be too bothered about the swelling and soreness of the arm, or the fever and weight loss, so she came to me, and asked if I would call round and examine him. The result of which is my having him admitted today.'

He walked over to the window to stand beside her and, with their shoulders almost touching, he said, 'The words "bone cancer" spring to mind, but let's wait and see.'

Claudia shuddered. He thought it might be one of the sarcomas. She could tell. If it was, she hoped that the boy would stand a better chance than Jack had.

That thought brought back once again the memory of life blood ebbing away on a beach in paradise and she bent her head in anguish.

'Come here, Claudia,' he said, drawing her to him. 'You don't have to be a toughie all the time.'

With her head against his chest she groaned. 'I'm not. That's the trouble. When I came back here everyone, including you, was so horrible to me that I decided I wasn't going to let you all see how much I was hurting. But it was all a sham, I'm afraid.'

She couldn't see his face but she could tell that he was smiling as he said, 'So you're not the slick chick you'd have me believe?'

'No. Not really. But *you* haven't been putting on an act, have you?'

'That depends on what you mean.'

'You *are* what you seem to be. The man who, because he had to fight his way to the top, hasn't much time for the likes of me, but has all the time in the world for Marina Beauchamp.'

'She needs me,' he said, his voice tightening. 'You must be blind if you can't see that…and I never refuse to go where I'm needed, even if it were to the ends of the earth.'

'Is that a threat or a promise?' she asked, slipping back into the role that she'd just admitted was a sham.

'It was neither,' he said coldly. 'Just as this isn't meant to be either of those things,' and, bending his head, he kissed her with a cool deliberation that made her try to fight him off. But he ignored the futile pummelling of her fists against his chest and continued with his onslaught on her senses.

As her struggles became less and her desire for him increased, Claudia knew that *she* needed him too, needed him desperately. But there was no way that she was going to tell him so. Not when he thought he could do what he liked with her...*and* had the attractive widow waiting on the sidelines.

The click of Belinda's heels on the passage outside had Lucas reluctantly releasing her and when her friend appeared in the doorway Claudia said desperately, 'I'll get back to the wards, if that's all right with you.'

'Yes, do that,' he agreed. 'I'll be back there myself shortly as I want to have a word with Jess Richardson with regard to the tests that I'm arranging for Peter.'

'It's fortunate that Marina is employed here. She'll be able to see him whenever she gets the chance.'

She'll be able to see *you* too, Claudia thought glumly. Yet, working in the same building, she'd always been able to do that. But, strangely, it was only now that Marina had appeared on the scene.

When Claudia had gone Lucas went to sit behind his desk, and once Belinda had left with the paperwork that she'd come to collect he allowed himself to reflect on Claudia Craven and her reactions to him.

There was chemistry between them, no doubt about that, but she still had the idea that he was hard and unfeeling and it made him not want to disappoint her.

Yet, unless he was completely crazy, he should be striving to make her see him in a different light. Though why should he? He'd always lived by the rule that if those he met didn't like him for what he was...too bad.

Marina Beauchamp had no such doubts about him. He could tell that. Life with her would be so much simpler. But when had he ever opted for the simple life?

As if to answer that question the phone rang at that moment and he recognised the voice at the other end as coming from an expensive nursing home on the Sussex coast. During the conversation that followed he knew more than ever that *his* life would never be uncomplicated.

When Claudia got home that night the day's earlier happenings were uppermost in her mind.

First there'd been the shock of discovering that the woman who'd seemed so close to Lucas was the mother of a prospective patient.

Then she'd found that her intuition regarding the consultant and the social worker hadn't been wrong. He'd even given her a lecture on how much Marina Beauchamp needed him, which had been followed by the humiliating switch of attention to herself...as if she were a tempting carrot dangling in front of him.

It had all been devastating to her peace of mind and out of it had come the realisation that she was falling in love with the last person on earth she would have chosen. .

When the bell rang at half-past ten and Claudia opened the door to find Lucas standing there, it really did seem as if there was nothing left to amaze her.

'I know,' he said before she could speak. 'I'm the last person you would expect to see at this hour...or want to, but as I was driving in this direction I thought I'd tell you what I have to say in person rather than phoning.'

'Come in,' she croaked, surprise affecting her throat muscles as well as her mind.

'Yes. I will…but only briefly.' His face looked gaunt in the lamplight in her elegant hallway and she knew miserably that he hadn't come to pledge undying love.

'I'm on my way to Worthing,' he said. 'My mother is in a nursing home there. I had a phone call earlier to say she wasn't well and the home have just rung again to say she's had a stroke.'

Claudia stared at him. 'Your mother! I didn't know that she was still alive. I'm so sorry, Lucas. How bad is it?'

'Bad enough, from all accounts. Mum has Alzheimer's. She's been in there two years. She lived with me before that but when it got really bad I had to let her go.'

'Dear me!' she exclaimed. 'You poor man.'

That brought a smile to his face. 'I never thought I'd live to see the day. Claudia Craven having kind thoughts about me! But I must go. What I came to say is…if the X-rays and bone biopsy I have arranged for Peter Beauchamp point towards some sort of bone cancer in the humerus, I want you to have further tests done, such as CT scanning of the lungs and radionuclide scanning of the rest of him. All of this is because I don't know how long I'll be in Worthing and I don't want there to be any delays with Marina's boy.'

'I'll follow your instructions to the letter,' she promised, while thinking that Marina really had got Lucas looking out for her and her son.

But that wasn't fair, was it? He would show the same degree of concern over any child with a possibly horrendous illness, and if in this case he was also very friendly with the parent, it was no business of hers.

'Drive carefully,' she said as he went out into the cold night.

His smile was mocking. 'All this concern is making me nervous. I'm not used to it.' And with that parting shot, he went.

Lucas had been right about Peter Beauchamp. The X-rays and biopsy showed that he had Ewing's sarcoma, a form of cancer found mostly in children between ten to fifteen years of age.

As soon as the results came through Claudia arranged for the further tests to be done that Lucas had ordered, so that they might discover if the cancer had spread, and in the meantime she needed to know from him what type and degree of medication should be given.

She'd had the task of telling Peter's mother what they had found, wishing as she'd done so that Lucas might have been there to have done it himself, as she felt sure that Marina Beauchamp's devastation would have been easier to bear if she'd had his support.

'Where *is* Lucas?' she'd wailed.

'He's had to go to see his mother who is seriously ill,' Claudia had explained gently, 'and has left me to arrange for further tests on your son.'

'To see if the cancer has spread?'

There'd been no use denying it.

'Yes. We need to know what we're up against, but do please remember that many cases like this are cured with radiotherapy and anti-cancer drugs. The success rate is very good. Sixty-five per cent of those who develop this type of cancer are still alive after five years and continue to stay well.'

The success rate hadn't been good in Jack's case, but that wasn't to say that it wouldn't be so for Marina's son, and Jack's *had* been a different type of cancer.

But first they had to see if the sarcoma had spread and

Claudia was hoping that by the time they got the results Lucas would be back to deal with the situation himself.

She wasn't comfortable with this woman who seemed to be so much closer to him than she was. Marina's degree of dependency on him was worrying, as it could so soon become a permanent thing and he *had* said that he preferred to be where he was needed. But surely he wouldn't take on the responsibility for Marina and her son out of compassion?

Yet it didn't have to be compassion. It was possible that he was in love with the woman. She was attractive enough to stir the senses of any man...and maybe at last Lucas was about to tune into his own needs for a change.

It was two days since he'd called at her apartment on his way to Worthing and so far there had been no word from him, which Claudia decided must mean that he was either on his way back, or his mother was too ill for him to think of anything else.

Of late there was tenderness inside her every time she thought of him, instead of anger and aversion, and she admitted to herself that, whether she wanted it to be so or not, Lucas Morrison had become the focal point of her existence.

It wasn't an admission that brought peace of mind—far from it. After losing Jack she had felt that love only brought pain when it was snatched away as it had been from her. That the only way to avoid a repeat performance was to stay in a safe cocoon of non-involvement.

But had she done that? No! She'd let a man who was the exact opposite of Jack break down her defences with his positive approach to life, his integrity...and the tigerish charm that both attracted and unnerved her.

Of course, there was a solution to the confusion of mind and heart that he had created in her. She could stay away from him. Not inside Lizzie's, obviously, unless she transferred to another hospital and she would be loth to do that.

The huge throbbing core of the place held her in thrall just as much as Lucas Morrison did, but there was nothing complicated about her relationship with the famous hospital. She knew where she was with Lizzie's.

It was in the other areas of her life that she needed to stay clear of Lucas if she wanted to avoid further hurt, but had she the strength of will to do that?

It transpired that he *was* on his way back. He appeared on the ward in the late afternoon of that same day, and when she saw him come through the door Marina left her son's bedside and flung herself sobbing into his arms.

Claudia eyed them anxiously. She hoped he was going to tell Marina that it wasn't going to do the boy any good if she kept on like that. Peter was distressed enough without having to witness his mother cracking up in front of him.

She needn't have worried. Lucas quickly guided her outside to the corridor and Claudia was left to take Peter's attention off what his mother and the consultant were doing and saying.

After a few seconds Lucas appeared without Marina and said briefly, 'Marina has gone for a cup of tea. So put me in the picture, please, Dr Craven.'

She wanted to ask how his mother was, but something told her it wasn't the right moment. Whether the reception he'd received from Marina Beauchamp had thrown him, or he was traumatised by something else, she didn't know, but he had withdrawn behind his professionalism.

When she'd finished doing as he'd asked Lucas said, 'I don't want to start treatment until we have the results from the radionuclide substance that's been injected into Peter's bloodstream. It will send off gamma rays and when the camera picks them up we'll have a better picture of what's happening with regard to the cancer.'

'His mother isn't coping very well,' Claudia said carefully, in an attempt to get behind the barrier he was putting up.

'So I see,' he replied. 'Which is only natural, I suppose, but Marina has to start thinking about the boy instead of herself. He needs her.'

And *she* needs you, Claudia thought glumly.

'When did you get back?' she asked, still wary of his brusque manner.

'I came straight here...and in case you're wondering...my mother died yesterday.'

His face was expressionless, his tone abrupt, but his eyes were moist and she wanted to take him in her arms and comfort him, yet it was neither the time or the place.

Lucas was his own man. Strong and indefatigable, he would no doubt cope with this as he did with everything else and *she* wouldn't be needed.

That was a thought that stayed with her until late in the afternoon when she had cause to seek Belinda out for a patient's notes.

When she knocked on the door of his office there was no reply, so she went in to find what she had come for, only to be rooted to the spot. Lucas was standing beside the window, dejection in every line of him, his shoulders shaking as harsh sobs tore at him.

At that moment Claudia forgot everything except the scene in front of her. He was lost and hurting. She had to comfort him.

With arms outstretched she moved towards him, dreading a rebuff, but when she whispered his name he turned blindly and went into them as if he knew it was where he belonged.

As she stroked his bowed head and the strong stem of his neck without speaking, his grief slowly spent itself and at last he looked up with the vestige of a smile on his lips.

'Why is it that you're always around in my moments of weakness?' he asked hoarsely. 'It's ruining my image.'

'Perhaps it's because it's where I want to be,' she said gently.

He was straightening up, flexing his shoulders. Any moment the man who needed her would be gone and the brisk surgeon would be back in his place.

She was right.

'Thanks, Claudia,' he said quietly. 'And now I must turn my attention to the living. Tell Robin Crawshaw that I want a word with him about the spinal injury that came in yesterday, will you?'

She was dismissed, but it didn't stop her from departing with the good feeling that came from being in the right place at the right time.

As she went back to the wards it seemed incredible to think that in a few short months she had reached a situation where the 'urban tiger' was seeking comfort in her arms, instead of snapping and snarling.

The glow inside her lasted until she was ready to leave for home an hour later and saw Lucas holding Marina in a close embrace on the corridor outside the wards.

Immediately she felt superfluous rather than supportive and went to seek out the Boxter with dragging steps.

The glow was still well and truly extinguished when she reported for duty the next day, but there was no time for moping. The roads outside were icy and treacherous.

Several fractures were requiring attention in theatre and on the wards.

Peter Beauchamp's results were through and there was rejoicing amongst the staff. The sarcoma hadn't spread. With radiotherapy and anti-cancer drugs the boy would have a good chance of recovery.

Even Sheila Newcome was smiling. She actually said, 'Good morning,' when Claudia appeared on the ward and impulsively the young doctor took her hand. 'I know you've a lot on your mind, Sheila,' she said, 'but I do hope we can be friends.'

'So do I,' the other woman said awkwardly. 'Maybe I have been a bit of a pain,' and on that note a truce was declared.

With the good news about Peter, Claudia was hoping that his mother might be less stressed and less in need of the attentions of Lucas. But if he was only too willing to be monopolised by Marina there wasn't much Claudia could do about it.

She had been wondering during the long hours of a restless night when his mother's funeral would be, and how much support the rest of his family were giving him and each other.

Lucas always seemed so alone, but who was to say that he didn't prefer it that way? He'd seen more than his share of the worst side of family life and perhaps he'd had enough.

The funeral was to be on the Saturday. He told her so the next morning as she and Robin did the ward rounds with him.

'There will just be myself, Sophie, Dimitri, Oliver, my young brother, and Craig...in his plaster casts,' he said levelly as his eyes flicked over a young patient's notes.

'It's to take place at a cemetery near the nursing home in Worthing.'

After that item of information it seemed that he had no further comments to make on his private affairs. As they moved from bed to bed he had only health matters to discuss.

When Lucas had gone striding off to wherever he was needed next, Robin said, 'He doesn't seem to be exactly heartbroken over his mother's death.'

'Don't be fooled by his manner. Lucas is devastated,' she told him, hoping that he wasn't going to ask how she came to be so well informed.

Robin would be dumbstruck if she were to tell him that Lucas had spilled out his grief in her arms. Yet she would never do that. It was a moment that belonged to her alone.

What it had meant to him she didn't know, but it had seemed that no sooner was it over than he was sharing an intimate embrace with Marina Beauchamp.

Claudia had made arrangements to go home that weekend and, even though she knew that Lucas would be very much on her mind, especially on the Saturday, there seemed no point in changing her plans.

She had no special place in his life. Her presence wasn't vital to him. He would have his family beside him at the funeral and would no doubt be his usual forceful self.

For all she knew he might have invited Marina to be beside him during the sad ceremony. If she was the widow of a friend of his their acquaintance must be of long standing, not a few brief months of alternating war and peace.

The large detached house, built from the golden stone of the Cotswolds, was bright and welcoming, her mother and father delighted to see her, and as she prepared to enjoy the brief respite Claudia vowed to put Lucas Morrison out of her mind.

That decision lasted until the moment her mother asked over afternoon tea, 'And how are you getting on with the Morrison man? Your description of him sounded quite ferocious.'

Her father had gone for a quick round of golf and there were just the two of them sitting comfortably beside a huge log fire.

Claudia looked away. Just the mere mention of his name made her heart skip a beat, but there had never been any secrets between herself and her mother, who was a fine-drawn, older version of herself, with the same golden hair, bright blue eyes and kind mouth.

'I was wrong about him, Mum,' she said ruefully. 'Lucas *can* be a bit intimidating sometimes, but it's because he's led a life so different from mine. It's made him hard and often on the defensive, but underneath all that he is quite a man. Caring and generous with his family, totally dedicated to his patients...'

'And?'

'Not exactly falling over himself to tie the nuptial knot with anyone.'

'Which is what you'd like him to do with you?' her mother questioned gently.

'Yes,' she admitted shamefully. 'Can you believe it? I've fallen in love with another man while I was still grieving for Jack. I feel ashamed...as if I didn't care enough.'

Tears hung on her mother's lashes. 'Don't feel like that, Claudia,' she said. 'As long as he is worthy of you it is the best thing that could have happened. You are young and beautiful. Jack wouldn't want you to be bogged down with grief for evermore. This is the news that your father and I have longed to hear. That the scars are healing and you're ready to get on with your life.'

'It isn't going to be as easy as that,' Claudia explained flatly. 'Lucas isn't in love with me. It's a one-sided affair. He's attracted to me in a haphazard sort of way, but we'd have a long way to go before it became a relationship. In any case, there is someone else that he's very close to.'

'But I thought you said that he wasn't interested in a permanent arrangement with anyone?'

'This is different. He's known her for some time. She's a widow with a teenage son, Peter, who's suffering from cancer at this moment.'

'I see, and because he's a caring man you think that Lucas might see this woman in a different light to yourself.'

'He does. I'm just the lucky little rich girl that he has reluctantly decided might one day be a good doctor. I feel as if that is all he will ever see me as.'

'Time will tell, Claudia,' her mother soothed. 'But if you want this man, let him see it. Show him that you care.'

CHAPTER FIVE

INSTEAD of driving back from Gloucestershire on the Sunday night Claudia left it until Monday morning. It meant being up at the crack of dawn but she was loath to leave the tranquillity of her parents' house for the uncertainty of her life in London.

Yet she knew she couldn't hide away, that Lizzie's wouldn't have disappeared overnight and neither would Lucas Morrison. Much as she had this reluctance to go back, she wouldn't want them to, as they were both in her blood.

The hospital, because of its sense of purpose, its dedication, its key awareness of the needs of children. And the man...because, single-minded though he might be, his values were the same.

Though there was more to her feelings for Lucas than that. His dark, mesmeric attractiveness, quicksilver mind, and the lithe grace of him were all part of the fascination that had her securely in its grip.

In spite of the early start Claudia was late in arriving due to long queues on the motorway. As she hurried past the still-shuttered shopping outlets in the hospital's main entrance she was feeling fraught and edgy because the day had started off on the wrong foot.

And it was not to improve. As she went to grab a quick coffee she found that the machine wasn't working. The orthopaedics unit was short of Jess Richardson who had phoned in to say she'd got a flu bug. Robin was less than his usual cheerful self due to a hangover from a party he'd been to the previous night. But most depressing of all there was no sign of Lucas, who was usually making his presence felt by eight o'clock.

How was he feeling today? she wondered. Relieved that the ordeal of the funeral was over? Or bereft at the finality of it? Whatever it was, now that she was back she couldn't wait to see him. Out there in the Cotswolds she'd held at bay the effect he had on her, but back inside the beating heart of Lizzie's the sight of him was as necessary as breathing.

'He's around somewhere,' Robin said. 'Try the social workers' office.'

'No way,' she snapped. If that was where he wanted to be at the beginning of a busy Monday morning he could get on with it.

There were no obvious emergencies regarding Peter. He had settled into the routine of the ward and was taking the medication and radiotherapy sessions without complaint. Within a few days he would be discharged and would continue the treatment as an outpatient, and so if Lucas was seeking Marina Beauchamp out it must be because he wanted to, rather than because he had to.

'So, what happened to you this morning?' his voice said from behind when she was walking down the corridor between the two wards, thinking dismal thoughts.

'I was foolish enough to think I could get here on time with a dawn start,' she told him flatly, 'but reckoned without a series of hold-ups on the motorway.'

'Had a nice weekend, then?'

'Yes. I won't ask you the same question.'

'No, don't. The funeral went according to plan. When it was over I came back home and brought young Oliver with me. He has no lectures for a couple of days so he's staying with me until Wednesday.'

'That's nice for you both. In times of sorrow it's good to have the support of one's family.'

It was true, but Claudia was aware that she sounded stilted and over polite. In fact they were both behaving like restrained acquaintances.

His glance had gone beyond her and she saw his mouth open in surprise for a second, then he was saying, 'Talk of the devil...here he is.'

As Claudia turned she saw a young man approaching. He was of average height, slender, and possessed a watered-down version of Lucas's striking looks.

To a teenage girl he would probably be seen as 'cool' in his designer clothes and with his close-cut hair, but to her he looked like someone out of Boyzone.

'My brother, Oliver,' Lucas said drily as he approached, and to the newcomer who was eyeing Claudia with obvious interest, 'Meet Dr Claudia Craven, a member of my team.'

'Hi, there,' Oliver said, and to his brother, 'You never told me there were doctors who looked like this!'

Claudia turned away to hide a smile as Lucas told him tectchily, 'Don't be fatuous,' and in the same tone, 'What are you doing here? When I left you sleeping I wasn't expecting you to surface before lunch-time.'

'I'm meeting some of the mates that I used to knock around with. We're going for a bevvy. Is that all right? Do I have your permission...big brother?'

Lucas sighed. 'You certainly have my permission to be on your way. We have work to do.'

'Sure thing,' he said easily, and to Claudia, 'You're welcome to join us. We'll be in the—'

'I said on your way, Oliver,' Lucas reminded him grimly.

When his young brother had obeyed his orders Lucas

said, 'I think I can just about suffer his presence until Wednesday. After that I wouldn't be responsible.'

She was laughing. 'He's typical of his age. Carefree, trendy, thinks he's God's gift to the opposite sex.'

'I suppose next to me he must seem like a breath of fresh air?'

That made her laugh even more. 'Next to you, he's pale and insignificant.'

'You really think so?' he asked softly.

Serious now, she eyed him warily. Where was the conversation leading? She'd been half teasing, even though she'd meant every word.

'Yes, I do.'

'In other words I'm pretty overpowering?'

'I've thought so…yes.'

'So, where does that leave us?'

'I don't know where it leaves you, but it leaves me very confused.'

'In what way?'

'I lost someone I loved dearly just a short time ago and I wanted to stay faithful to his memory.'

'And is something stopping you?'

'Yes, but why ask? You know what I'm talking about.'

They were standing beside an arrangement of tall trees and shrubs, so arranged in tubs to make a small oasis of greenery amongst the tiles and gloss paint of the corridor, and, on seeing that there was no one about, Lucas drew her to one side so that they were hidden from view by the plants.

Taking her face between his hands, he said softly, 'Is this the kind of thing that's confusing you?'

No sooner had the words left his lips than he was placing his mouth on hers. His arms were around her and he was moulding her soft curves against the male hardness of him as he kissed her with swift urgency.

Whether it was because someone might come along at any moment and see them, or because he was experiencing a sudden flare-up of passion, she didn't know, but to Claudia the day that had started off so depressingly was brightening by the minute. His lips were nuzzling her throat now, his hands cupping her taut breasts, and it was there again, the sweet desire that made anything she'd ever felt before seem as nothing.

'They'll be sending out a search party for us,' he said at last, '*and* I've made a commitment to see Marina Beauchamp. We need to talk, Claudia. Let's meet somewhere tonight.'

'You have some nerve!' she said angrily as the moment disintegrated. 'Dragging me behind the potted palms for a quick bout of passion. Then in the next breath telling me that what I've suspected all along is true. That you've got something going with someone else. Don't ever touch me again!'

The corridor was still deserted and as she strode off, ignoring his harsh command to 'Stop being so stupid,' she was offering up a prayer of thanks because incredibly in the middle of busy Lizzie's no one had been around to witness her humiliation.

When she appeared back on the wards Robin eyed her curiously. 'Where have you been?' he wanted to know. 'Miles Soper has just put in an appearance and is looking for Lucas and I've been trying to find you.'

'Why? What's wrong?' she asked edgily.

'Nothing. It's time for the ward rounds and I'm always happier when we do them together.'

'I'm sorry,' she said apologetically. 'I allowed myself

to be waylaid...but you can rest assured it won't happen again.'

It had been to herself, rather than Robin, that she'd been emphasising that it wasn't going to happen again. In those first weeks of getting to know Lucas Morrison she'd had the impression that, although he was disturbingly attractive in a saturnine sort of way, the man was not a womaniser— either because he was too engrossed in the job, or because he was bogged down with family commitments...or both.

Since then she'd discovered that he was not immune to the needs, in whatever form they presented themselves, of the wife of an old friend, and was also not averse to having a quick dalliance with herself whenever the opportunity presented itself.

A circumstance that might not be so disturbing if she was on the lookout for a quick kiss and cuddle, but she wasn't the type to spread her favours around casually.

She'd known Jack since they were both teenagers. Quiet and uncomplicated, with a quizzical sense of humour, the lanky marine biologist, his colouring as golden as her own, had been her choice.

Whether that would have remained so if Lucas Morrison had walked into her life sooner, she didn't know, but she had an instinctive feeling that, no matter when or where they'd met, falling in love with him was inevitable, which wasn't a thought that brought much joy with it. Not at that precise moment, anyway.

When she and Robin stopped beside the bed of five-year-old Sally Haynes the physiotherapist was coaxing the little girl to do some gentle exercises to relieve swollen and painful joints.

Lucas had seen the child two weeks previously in his clinic and had had her admitted to the unit immediately.

She had been suffering from joint problems for the last two months along with intermittent fever, stomach pains, and there had been some weight loss.

On examination he had found her to have enlarged lymph nodes and a lot of pain in the knee and elbow joints.

He had discussed her case with the two junior doctors at the time, explaining that the symptoms could come from various causes such as Crohn's disease, ulcerative colitis, or even leukaemia, but results from tests done shortly after admission had shown that none of those illnesses was present.

The findings had pointed to juvenile rheumatoid arthritis—polyarticular. Tests done to check inflammation of the joints had shown a high ESR—erythrocyte sedimentation rate—of 55mm per hour. There had also been some anaemia and a degree of osteoporosis of the hands present.

Lucas had prescribed aspirin, always the first choice in such cases, to maintain therapeutic blood levels, while at the same time giving pain relief. He had arranged for night splints to be worn to prevent any deformities and to keep the joints comfortable.

As Sally's stay at Lizzie's could be for a few weeks she was attending the hospital school, much to her delight and the relief of her parents, who were grateful for anything that might take the little girl's mind off her discomfort.

However, at this moment she wasn't very happy as the physiotherapist did her job. She was making little whimpering noises and her bottom lip was jutting out mutinously.

'What is it, Sallykins? Is it hurting?' Lucas's voice said from behind.

She nodded and gave an aggrieved sniffle at the same time.

'You do know that this will help to make it better, don't

you?' he said gently. 'And once we've got your arms and
legs more comfortable you'll be able to go home...and
guess what?'

'What?' she asked with another sniffle.

'You know how you love school?'

'Er...yes?'

'Well, when you go home you will have a teacher all
to yourself. She will come to your house to teach you until
you're better. What do you think about that?'

The physiotherapist had stepped back at his arrival and
all the while he'd been chatting to the little girl Lucas had
been examining her.

When he had finished he turned to the two doctors and
said briefly, 'Your turn. What improvement is there...if
any?'

'Not a lot,' Robin said when he'd conducted his own
examination.

'And what does Dr Craven think?' Lucas asked as
Claudia did likewise.

'I agree with Robin,' she said stiffly. 'Could the aspirin
be increased?'

'Maybe. Or I might prescribe something else.'

'Such as?' she questioned, deciding that he wasn't the
only one who could be sparse of speech when they felt
like it.

He was eyeing her levelly. 'You tell me.'

'Penicillamine, chloroquine?'

'Not in this case,' he answered coldly. 'If you'd taken
the trouble to read Sally's notes you would be aware that
her condition isn't so bad that she needs anti-rheumatic
drugs.'

Claudia could feel her colour rising. Had she boobed?
Or was it a case of the swords being out?

'I've read the notes,' she told him defiantly, and, taking

them from the clip at the bottom of the bed, she scanned them quickly. She was certain that she'd seen written there that if aspirin didn't do the trick he would try...

Her face took on a deeper hue. He had suggested anti-inflammatory drugs as a second choice...not the more powerful anti-rheumatic compounds.

'Well?'

'You're right,' she admitted. 'I must have misread your instructions.'

'You misread a lot of things, Dr Craven,' he said in the same tone, and with a nod to the transfixed Robin he strode off in the direction of the other ward.

'Phew!' he said as they moved on. 'What was all that about? I was under the impression that Morrison sees you as God's new gift to orthopaedics. What have you done to annoy him to that extent?'

'Nothing,' she replied grimly. 'I made a mistake and he pounced on it.'

'But it's not like you to do anything like that,' he protested.

'I'm only human, the same as everybody else, Robin. I don't possess magic powers of memory and observation.'

Her new friend, Sheila Newcome, was listening and she butted in, 'Lucas did say something about anti-rheumatic drugs when Sally was first admitted, but, when her condition wasn't as serious as he'd thought it might be, he changed his mind. Maybe what he said had stuck in your mind, Claudia.'

Claudia smiled. It was worth being in trouble with Lucas to have the redoubtable Sheila on her side and she gave the plump nurse a hug.

'Thanks for that, Sheila,' she said, 'Even though it doesn't let me off the hook with Lucas.'

The other woman was frowning. 'I wonder why he's so

grumpy. He was all right when he came in first thing. But he's been to see the glamorous Marina since then. Maybe all is not sweetness and light in those quarters.'

'Maybe,' Claudia murmured casually.

It was in her own quarters where the sweetness and light was lacking, she thought, but there was no way she was going to acquaint Sheila with that titbit.

If the nurse and Robin thought that Lucas was taking it out on her because of some sort of misunderstanding with the sultry widow it was simpler to let them go on thinking it. Only she knew that Lucas and herself had been in each other's arms just a short time ago. As usual it had been a non-event for Lucas and, instead of it being herself who had cause to be less than pleased, he was getting his displeasure in first.

It had been merely a slip of the tongue, a misunderstanding, and he had nearly jumped down her throat. The fact that ninety-nine per cent of the time she was totally efficient hadn't counted for anything.

Claudia was alone in the restaurant during the lunchhour. Robin had gone to have his hair cut, an event of some interest amongst the staff, as he was about to dispense with the shoulder-length, lank brown locks for a shorter, more fashionable cut.

When she looked up and saw Lucas in the queue she quickly averted her eyes and went on with her meal as if her life depended on it.

'Where's "boy wonder"?' his voice said from behind her some seconds later, and as Claudia reluctantly lifted her eyes from her plate he settled himself in the seat opposite.

'Gone to have his hair cut,' she said briefly.

'Not before time!' he said with a surprised lift of dark brows.

'The length of Robin's hair isn't really anyone else's business, is it?' she commented stonily.

'It is if the sight of a long-haired hippy appearing at their bedside creates a lack of confidence amongst the patients.'

Claudia glared at him. He was really out to needle her today. Those moments behind the greenery had made her think that it wasn't going to be such a bad day after all, but from the second that he had brought her crashing back to earth it had gone from bad to worse.

'If I were a patient I would be more interested in the standard of care a doctor was offering than the length of his hair. Even though some of us aren't as on the ball as you would like.'

'Still rankling, is it…your mistake over Sally's treatment?'

'Yes.'

'Would it make you feel better if I were to tell you that I *had* expected to have to use the anti-rheumatic drugs and had probably discussed it with you previously?'

'It would make little difference to the way I feel, I'm afraid,' she told him as it registered that Sheila had been right in what she'd said. 'I know that in the medical profession we can't afford to make mistakes, but we were merely having a discussion about a patient's treatment and I said the wrong thing. I wasn't about to prescribe something I wasn't sure about. Yet you pounced on me as if I was totally incompetent.'

'Would it make any difference if I said I'm sorry? That I was suffering from post-traumatic Claudia Craven syndrome?'

'And how do you think *I* was feeling at the time? I know that you see me as a bit of light entertainment to liven up the working day…but that isn't how I see you.'

'How do you see me, Claudia?' he said with sudden tight urgency. As she opened her mouth he put out a restraining hand. 'No. Don't tell me now. You can tell me tonight. I said we needed to talk. Remember?'

'Yes, you did, but I don't remember agreeing.'

He ignored the sarcasm as if she hadn't spoken.

'Your place? Or mine?'

'Yours,' she suggested, unable to resist the temptation of seeing him in his own place.

Lucas was smiling now that she'd capitulated. 'You're sure that you want to go slumming?'

'Your place can't be any worse than some of the accommodation we stayed in on our world trip.'

His smile was fading. 'That is all still very much to the front of your mind, isn't it?'

'Well, of course it is. What would you expect? That I've forgotten I lost someone I loved during that time?'

'No, of course not,' he said tonelessly.

'So what time shall we say?' she asked before the conversation got into any deeper waters.

'Seven-thirty? And don't eat before you come. I'll cook us a meal.'

'Er…yes…all right,' Claudia agreed doubtfully. It was only a couple of hours since she'd decided to stay clear of him and here she was agreeing to a cosy evening with the urban tiger. And wasn't it typical that, added to all his other talents, he could cook? Or maybe he was just good with a tin-opener.

If she'd been expecting Lucas to appear in a plastic apron, with a cook's hat on his head, and waving a wooden spoon when she rang his doorbell, Claudia was due for a disappointment.

He looked cool and unruffled and his casual shirt and

jeans had a designer look about them. So it had to be the tin-opener, she decided.

As he took her coat Claudia was aware that if his abode was average hospital accommodation from the outside, it was a tasteful bachelor apartment once over the threshold, furnished with good furniture, elegant curtains, and warm-looking rugs on a polished wooden floor.

'Very nice!' she murmured admiringly.

'An improvement on what you expected, is it?' he asked with familiar irony.

'Nothing is how I imagine it will be, where you're concerned,' she said. 'You never cease to confound me.'

'I suppose I could take that as a compliment,' he parried as he put a drink in her hand, 'though I'm positive it wasn't meant as one. Let's keep it light, shall we, Claudia? No soul-searching tonight?'

She shrugged. 'Whatever you say, but I was under the impression that you wanted us to talk seriously about something or other.'

'Er…well…yes, I do, but let's eat first, shall we?'

'Whatever you say.'

'For God's sake, stop repeating yourself…and there's no need to be so meek,' he remonstrated. 'It doesn't suit you.'

'Fine. I'll bear that in mind. Maybe you'd like to tell me what does suit me?'

'I could do that, but you mightn't appreciate it.'

'Why not try me?'

He was moving in the direction of the kitchen. 'No more questions. If you're not hungry, I am.'

'Are you expecting your brother to join us?' she called after him.

'Oliver? No. He's still out somewhere with his friends. I'll be lucky if I see him this side of midnight.'

'Don't you ever get lonely?'

'Why do you ask?'

The answer to that was because she cared, but she could just see him dropping the plates that he was carrying in from the kitchen were she to tell him so.

'You're dealing with the public all day and on your own at night.'

'The same applies to you,' he said with bland reasoning.

'Yes, but mine is from choice.'

'And you think mine wasn't?'

'I notice you're speaking in the past tense. Does that mean you are about to change your lifestyle?'

Lucas was pulling a chair away from the table for her and as she seated herself it was clear that he did know how to cook. Yet there had been no clutter visible in the kitchen, no cooking smells. Grilled steaks and fresh vegetables did usually have an aroma of their own, unless they'd been cooked elsewhere.

His smile as he read her thoughts had a certain puckish wickedness about it. 'All right. I admit it. I did have the food brought in, but only because I was so late getting home there was no time to cook it myself.'

He had seated himself opposite and as they began to eat he said, 'You asked if I was about to change my lifestyle? The answer to that is "maybe". It depends on someone else.'

'The commitment to Marina Beauchamp that you referred to?'

'That could affect me. But there are other things pulling at me too.'

'Such as?' Claudia questioned softly, not daring to hope that what she wanted to hear was coming next.

It wasn't.

'You know that I don't practise private medicine?'

'Yes.' The monosyllable had come forth as flat as the floor beneath her feet.

'Well, a wealthy Arab businessman has approached Lizzie's regarding an orthopaedic problem affecting one of his sons. My name has been put forward and he wants me to operate.'

'That sounds a trifle tricky,' she remarked, interested in spite of being disappointed at the impersonal nature of the subject.

Lucas shrugged his shoulders as if he had no qualms in that respect. 'He's to take over one of the private suites at St Elizabeth's for his son, and the entourage that travels around with them has been booked into a top London hotel.'

'And have you agreed to perform the surgery?'

'Yes, in this instance, and as you've worked with me before in theatre I've included you in the team.'

'So you don't think I'm too incompetent?'

'Why? Because of this morning? I'm afraid that was an instance of male pique.'

'If anyone should be piqued about that, it's me,' Claudia told him, amazed that this man, of all people, was prepared to admit he might be less than perfect. 'You know that I'm not immune to your particular kind of charm and you take advantage of it, even though you're in cahoots with someone else.'

He was frowning now and Claudia thought bleakly that he was willing to allow a degree of self-criticism, but it didn't go down well coming from someone else.

'I've known Marina Beauchamp and her son for a long time, if that is what you're referring to. Her husband was in the regular army and was a casualty of the Ulster conflicts. He asked me to be there for them if anything happened to him. Naturally I agreed, but until recently they had never needed me. Now they do. Just like your friend Jack needed you. It's as simple as that.'

Simple! she wanted to shriek. What's simple about it? I'm in love with you. You're in love with her. Or are you? Are you carrying the essence of chivalry to ridiculous lengths?

Lucas was bending over her to refill her glass and as she looked up at him their glances held, his the dark mirror for his thoughts, hers bright, blue, and challenging.

Locked in the moment neither of them heeded the wine spilling over the top of the glass to slide across the table in a dark red tide.

'You're too beautiful for your own good, Claudia Craven,' he said huskily. 'You keep interfering with the plans I've made.'

'In what way?' she asked softly.

'This way,' he breathed, and, putting the bottle down amongst the spilt wine, he bent to kiss her. As their mouths made contact Claudia got to her feet and, with her arms around his neck, kissed him back with a fervour that had him saying raggedly, 'Whoa! Where do we go from here?'

She was about to tell him that the answer to that had to come from him when she heard a key being turned in the lock, followed by his brother's voice calling from the outer hall, 'It's me, bro. Anything left to eat?'

'Damn! What's he doing here?' Lucas hissed. 'He *never* comes in this early!'

Claudia had sunk back onto her chair and was mopping up the spilt wine as if her life depended on it when Oliver appeared in the doorway.

'Ah!' he said. 'So you have a visitor. Shall I make myself scarce again?'

'No! Of course not!' Lucas gritted, and if she hadn't

been feeling so put out too she would have wanted to laugh.

Claudia supposed she should be grateful that the laid-back student had brought them back to earth, had stopped the fever that had gripped them again from reaching a dangerous pitch, but for now she could only wish he'd stayed away.

Having put a blight on their evening, Oliver wandered off into the kitchen to forage for the food that he'd mentioned, leaving Lucas and herself to casual chit-chat about hospital matters and life in general, but it was difficult to behave normally after the high emotions before Oliver had come back and after a little while she got up to go.

'I'm sorry that young Ollie butted into our evening,' he said as he reached into the hall closet for the black jacket that was part of the smart trouser suit she'd chosen to wear. 'We must do it again, as there are still a lot of things unsaid between us.'

'Anything you had to say to me could have been said long before your brother turned up,' she pointed out with cool reason. 'Maybe he did you a favour. He certainly did me one.'

'I see,' Lucas said coldly, his face darkening. 'Why do I keep thinking that your mind is running along the same lines as mine? I must be crazy.'

'Your life runs along tracks of your own making,' she said, stepping out onto the landing outside his door. 'There aren't many folk who could keep up with you. I certainly can't.'

As she drove back to her apartment Claudia felt gloom descending. The evening had been a jumble of untied ends, unspoken thoughts and desires and double-talk. She had a sudden longing for the company of someone uncomplicated.

Robin lived in one of the blocks near Lucas. Would he be in? she wondered. The only way to find out was to turn the car round and knock on his door.

No sooner had the thought been born than the deed was done and as she rang his doorbell she was smiling at the thought of his expression when he saw her there.

She didn't see the tall figure watching her from the shadows thrown by a March moon, or watch him retrace his steps with shoulders hunched, his solitary stroll cut short by something he hadn't bargained to see.

Calling to see Robin turned out to be a wasted exercise. There was no welcoming smile or cheery greeting for her because he wasn't in, and so once more Claudia set off for home, this time not allowing herself to be sidetracked.

It was a good description of how her life seemed to be at present: sidetracked. And who was to blame? Only herself if she kept making herself available every time Lucas Morrison crooked his finger.

CHAPTER SIX

THE flowing robes of Omar Al Saud made a bright splash of colour on a March morning as he eased himself out of the first of the three limousines that had glided to a halt outside the front entrance of St Elizabeth's.

As he stood looking around him the wealthy Arab was followed by the slight figure of his son and two burly attendants, while from the second and third cars emerged the female members of the party.

Looking down on them from a ward window on a higher level, Claudia wondered which of the shrouded figures on the street below was the boy's mother.

One of the women, or maybe more, if the grandmother and aunts were present, would be in just as great a state of anxiety as their western counterparts would be on such an occasion, but without the opportunity to voice it as freely.

She had a clear view of the child from where she was watching and saw that eleven-year-old Ibrahim Saud was doing the same as his father, looking around him with bright dark eyes in a brown face, capped by the black locks so common to his race.

As the party began to move forward with the women at the rear, Claudia saw something else: the boy had a pronounced limp.

She knew that Lucas and one of the managers of the hospital trust were waiting to welcome them in the glass-covered entrance hall, and from there the Arab and his entourage would be escorted to the private suite of rooms where the boy was to be treated.

'Why do you think Lucas is doing this?' Robin had questioned when he'd heard about the private patient who'd been shortly to arrive at Lizzie's. 'Is it for the cash, do you think?'

'I shouldn't think so,' she'd said. 'We both know that lots of overseas people send their children to Lizzie's for private treatment and the consultants attend them on that basis. It isn't the same as him having a private practice somewhere.

'As far as Lucas is concerned, he relates to any child with a bone problem, whether rich or poor, and if in this instance the child is from a very wealthy family who have asked him to perform the surgery...why not?'

'What's wrong with the boy?' Robin had persisted. 'You ought to know. You're the one he talks to. He can't take his eyes off you.'

'Huh! That's because he feels the need to check up on me after the mistake I made the other day.'

'*I've* done far worse things than that and he doesn't feel the need to watch me.'

Claudia had ignored that. 'He's going to do an osteotomy. A fractured femur from a riding accident hasn't healed correctly and the boy has ended up with one leg shorter than the other.'

'So how is Lucas going to correct it? And why bring the kid all the way from Kuwait to St Elizabeth's when they must have their own hospitals over there?'

'The answer to the first question is that I don't know whether he's going to straighten the bone in the leg that was fractured, or shorten the good leg to make them equal. No doubt all will soon be revealed if we are to assist in theatre.'

She could have said that since the night she'd dined with Lucas and found it a very unsettling experience they'd had little to say to each other. He had been abrupt and uncommunicative except for the concerns of their patients.

It had occurred to her that he was regretting having created a situation where their relationship could have progressed and was now involved in a tactical retreat.

She could have also informed Robin that she'd called at his place that night for a dose of *his* uncomplicated company, only to find that he was out.

He'd waved a hand in front of her eyes. 'Wakey wakey! You're miles way, Claudia. What about the other thing I was querying? Why bring the boy here?'

'Yes...well...don't you think that Ibrahim's father might have decided that, as the surgeons in his own country didn't do too good a job when his son fractured his leg, it's worth bringing him to Lizzie's. After all, this place is known and revered all over the world. I've even heard a whisper that the royals have been putting out feelers with regard to one of their offspring being admitted for private treatment.'

And now the subject of their discussion had arrived and was at that moment being shown to the part of the hospital where he would be residing for the next couple of weeks.

In the meantime the work of the orthopaedic unit had to go on and, as if to confirm that, Lucas was with them within the hour asking for reports on the various children at present in their care.

He was pleasant enough with Robin but still aloof with herself and Claudia had to admit his attitude was making her miserable.

She would prefer anything to being kept at arm's length. Arguing, verbal sparring, battle of wits—anything would be better than this, she thought as he gave her brief instructions regarding a baby admitted with an ankle deformity.

There had been no signs of Marina Beauchamp on the ward recently, but there was a good reason for that. Peter had been discharged and would be seen by Lucas in his clinic from now on, which gave his mother no reason to present herself...unless her relationship with Lucas called for it.

Later in the day when he asked Claudia to accompany him to the private suite where the Al Saud family were now ensconced, she was only too happy to obey.

For one thing she was desperate for his company, frosty though it may be, and, for another, she was curious to meet the small patient and his relatives.

Omar Al Saud was seated in a large leather chair in a corner of the room, surveying those present with shrewd dark eyes, while a couple of the women scuttled to and fro, eyes apprehensive and watchful above the *chuddar*.

'Mr Al Saud, this is Dr Claudia Craven who will be assisting me when I operate on your son,' Lucas told him. 'I have asked her along so that she can examine him.'

The Arab nodded his gracious permission, and as Claudia moved towards the bed she was aware that another man had just entered the room.

He was taller than Omar Al Saud but he had the same natural arrogance of manner as the older man and there was a strong facial resemblance that made it no surprise when Omar introduced him as his eldest son, Faisal.

'I came on a later flight,' the newcomer told Lucas in the same concise English as his father's, but, though he was addressing the senior doctor, Claudia was aware that his eyes were on her, taking in the long golden sheen of her hair, and the shapely legs visible beneath the short hospital coat.

Lucas had also noted the direction of his glance and his face tightened, while Omar, still sitting regally in his vantage position in the corner, eyed his eldest son benignly.

I'm here to see the patient, Claudia thought mutinously, not to be looked over as if I'm 'goods for the sale of'!

Bending over the boy, she began to examine his legs and as he watched her with anxious dark eyes she said gently, 'Don't worry, Ibrahim. Dr Morrison is going to make you better.'

'That's right,' Lucas said from beside her. 'We're going to make you walk straight again, Ibrahim…and, I promise you, there is nothing to be afraid of.'

'I've had X-rays done already and it is the fractured femur that hasn't healed straight,' he told Claudia. 'The bone is curved, making that leg shorter than the other.

'Mr Al Saud is adamant that the other leg is not to be shortened to bring both limbs into line and I am in agreement. So I'm going to straighten the long bone…and Dr Crawshaw and yourself are going to assist me.'

'When is the operation to be?' she asked.

'Tomorrow. So make sure that you're available.'

If his tone had been mild while he'd been speaking to the boy, it wasn't so now that he was addressing herself, and when they left the room, with Claudia conscious that the young Arab's eyes were following her, she said stiffly, 'And where would you expect me to be? I'm always where I'm wanted…and sometimes where I'm not, if the cold zone that seems to form every time we're together is anything to go by.'

'I was meaning that Omar's eldest son was showing his appreciation of a fair-skinned woman.'

'So? What has that got to do with me?' she snapped.

'You might feel like a diversion. Or are you still extra chummy with "boy wonder"?'

Claudia stared at him. 'Who? Robin? Of course I'm "chummy", as you put it, with Robin! I know where I stand with him. He doesn't talk in riddles. He's a lovely fellow. And as for Faisal, what do you think I am? It doesn't mean that because you aren't attracted to me I have to fall for the first man I meet.'

Suddenly grave, and with no idea how that same gravity sat so touchingly on her, she told him, 'Jack was the only man I'd ever known. I'm not experienced in relationships with your sex. If I were, I might be feeling less unhappy.'

His face softened and he reached out and touched her cheek gently. 'Don't be unhappy, Claudia. You said that young Crawshaw is uncomplicated...a lovely fellow. If you're going to replace your Jack that's the kind of man you need. Not a hard-bitten, up-from-the-gutter type.'

Claudia felt tears prick. They were both victims. In different ways perhaps, but victims nevertheless. She was suffering from a situation over which she'd had no control and Lucas was the product of his upbringing: tough, decisive, and what?

Not lacking in love when it came to his family or the children he treated, but wary and on the defensive when it came to another kind of love—that of a man for a woman.

'I'll remember what you say,' she said quietly, 'but don't think that you are always right. The fact that I've taken note of your advice doesn't mean that I'm going to act on it.'

His face brightened and her heart skipped a beat. Maybe he hadn't meant it, had just been sounding her out, but when she looked up and saw Marina Beauchamp coming down the corridor towards them it seemed that here was the reason for his sudden rise in spirits.

'Now here is someone who's always welcome where you're concerned,' she said lightly. 'Just the person you need to brighten your day,' and with a brief smile for the other woman she went, back to Robin, Jess, Sheila, the rest of the staff on Orthopaedics…and reality.

Easter was in two weeks' time and Claudia hadn't made any definite plans for it as she would be working on good Friday and the Monday. It left two free days in the middle but for some reason she couldn't conjure up any enthusiasm with regard to what to do with them.

Her mother had asked if she was coming home but so far she hadn't committed herself. She'd heard Lucas telling someone that he was spending Good Friday with the Beauchamps and that had made her feel that they were as far apart as ever, but even if he hadn't been going there she would have been working, so what did it matter?

It did matter, though. It mattered a lot.

Faisal Al Saud was there, along with the rest of his family, when Lucas and she went to see Ibrahim before he was taken down to theatre, and Claudia was so aware of the heat of his elder brother's interest in her that it was like being scorched by fire. He had some nerve, she thought, sending out signals towards herself when the rest of his family were totally absorbed in the boy's problem.

Though she had a feeling that his father wasn't entirely unaware of what his son was up to and didn't disapprove, which made her wonder if Faisal's behaviour would be looked upon with favour no matter how he acted.

Lucas had again noted Faisal's interest in her and as they left the room to make their way to theatre he growled, 'If number one son doesn't take his eyes off you I shall feel like blacking them for him.'

She smiled up at him. 'Haven't we had this conversation before…and didn't I tell you that I'm not interested?'

It would have been nice to add, But it's good to know

that you can feel jealous on my account, just as I feel sick every time I think of you with Marina. Yet what was the point? Lucas might object to the warm-eyed Faisal's attentions, but it wasn't because he was panting for her himself.

Robin wasn't with them in theatre during the operation to correct Ibrahim's crooked leg. He'd been seconded to assist Miles Soper with a bad fracture that needed pinning, and so it was she and Lucas representing Orthopaedics along with the regular theatre team.

When the boy had been anaesthetised Lucas made an oblique cut in the deformed bone and, when ready to rejoin the two ends, placed them slightly out of line to bring the whole bone into a position where it would stay straight. Once that was done he fastened a metal plate to the corrected femur to hold it in position.

As Claudia looked, learned, and assisted generally, she was, as always, impressed with the skill and total concentration with which Lucas operated. Was he always wary of something going wrong, as perhaps it often had during his hard childhood? she wondered.

Or was it because nothing had ever been easy for Lucas that he was so thorough? And now, with the power to make things right for others, as no one had ever done for him, he was generous with his talents?

As they scrubbed up afterwards there was tenderness in her for the man that the underprivileged boy had become, and as he bent over the basin she touched the back of his neck gently with a soapy hand.

He looked up. 'Hey! What was that for?'

'Because I admire you more than anyone I know.'

'Oh. I see.'

Was it disappointment she could hear in his voice? What was he expecting her to say?

Whatever it was, he wasn't going to elaborate on it at that moment. 'Let's go and tell the Al Saud family that the deed is done and that their youngster is going to walk straight again.'

'You tell them,' she said. 'Omar Al Saud won't be interested in anything a junior doctor has to say.'

'What about the over-heated Faisal? I'm sure he'd like to see you.'

Still on a high after working with him, she smiled. 'Don't push it, Lucas. I can't see myself in the harem and I never did like hot countries.'

'And Goa in particular?'

She shuddered and waited for the pictures to start appearing in her mind, but this time they didn't come. There was only the face of the man beside her dominating her thoughts. No cries from the flea market at Anjuna, or red blood on yellow sand, just the knowledge that she was back to living again—but to what degree she was far from sure.

When Lucas asked her to spend Easter Saturday with him Claudia was dubious about accepting. Not because she wasn't desperate to be with him, but because there was a feeling inside her that this was to be her slot.

He'd fitted Marina in on the Friday and now it was her turn as the hanger-on, she thought. So instead of biting his hand off she asked coolly, 'Why? Why are you asking me to spend the day with you?'

Rolling his eyes heavenwards, he sighed. 'Do I have to give a reason? Can't we just say that we're both at a loose end and so might as well join company? Before I lost my mother I would have been spending the holiday weekend with her.'

'Yes, of course,' she murmured, reminding herself that his loss was very recent and that he must still be hurting a lot. 'Where do you suggest we go?'

'It's up to you. I'm easy.'

Claudia thought for a moment and then said hesitantly, 'Would it be too far if I suggested we pay my parents a brief visit?'

He surveyed her with raised brows and she hoped that he wasn't thinking she wanted to take him to be looked over, but it appeared that he wasn't thinking on those lines. Instead he said with his usual irony, 'Are you sure they'll want to meet a rough diamond like myself?'

'Don't be ridiculous!' she said tartly. 'You're not rough...but you do have the ability to dazzle, as does the diamond, and, Lucas, will you please stop comparing us? I don't know if you hanker after moulding me into a different kind of person that you would approve of more, but as far as I'm concerned I don't want *you* to change. So do stop harping about our different backgrounds, will you?'

When she finished speaking he eyed her thoughtfully for a moment and then said slowly, 'I will bear all of that in mind...and if that is how you really feel I shall be pleased to drive us to Gloucestershire.'

'You can't drive here and back in one day,' her mother exclaimed when Claudia phoned to tell her of their proposed visit. 'You must both stay the night.'

There was silence while Claudia thought about the suggestion. 'I'll have to check with Lucas first, Mum,' she said. 'He may have plans for the Sunday.'

'Such as?'

'I don't know. He has family that he is very supportive

of and also likes to be on hand for the widow of a friend of his and her son.'

'But he has time for you also?' her mother probed gently.

'Not in the true sense,' Claudia told her, 'so don't go getting ideas. We're driving down together because we are both at a loose end over Easter.'

'I see. Well, I'll wait until I hear from you again, but, whatever you decide, your dad and I would love to see you...*and* the intriguing man that you're bringing with you.'

When she told Lucas of her mother's suggestion he eyed her with the same thoughtfulness as when she'd first suggested they go up to visit her parents, and she wished she knew what he was thinking. But his hesitation was brief.

'Of course I don't mind staying overnight if your parents will have me,' he said. 'It's a beautiful part of the country. We'll be in April by then. Spring will be here. There will be new beginnings everywhere.'

For whom? she'd wanted to ask, but it was enough that they were going to spend two days together.

Ibrahim Saud was discharged from St Elizabeth's a couple of days before Easter and, although Claudia was sorry to see the enchanting small boy depart, it was a relief to know that his elder brother would no longer be bestowing his attentions upon her.

The operation had been a success and regular physiotherapy when he got home would soon have him walking naturally. It had been difficult for the two doctors to tell which of the women concealed behind the *chuddar* was his mother, but on the last day one of them had taken Claudia to one side and said shyly, 'I thank you for what you have done for my son. Please tell Dr Morrison of my thanks. Soon Ibrahim will be able to run with his brothers and sisters.'

Claudia had taken the woman's soft hand in hers. 'I will tell him,' she'd promised, 'and don't worry if the leg takes a little time to adjust.'

Lucas handled his old Rover as he did everything else: with confidence and purpose. There had been no mention of them travelling to Gloucestershire in the Boxter and Claudia had no wish to push it.

For one thing, she sensed that he wouldn't want to be driven to her parents' house, that he wouldn't want to be seen as the passenger, instead of in the driving seat. That was the way he was and, now that she understood him better, she loved him for it.

She dressed casually for the journey in a heavy-ribbed white sweater and tight-fitting blue jeans and now was snuggled down contentedly in the passenger seat as they left the London traffic behind and headed for the Cotswolds.

Expecting Lucas to be dressed in a similar manner, she was surprised to see that he was wearing a shirt, tie, and a smart jacket and trousers of fine tweed.

Obviously he felt the need to dress up, she thought. Surely he didn't think he had to make an impression? He would still be seen as someone special in a boiler suit and a cloth cap!

He'd seen the question in her eyes as she'd got in the car and had asked drily, 'Why are you looking at me like that?'

'Like what?'

'As if you're wondering if I've just stepped out of Simpson's window.'

She laughed. 'You look very smart.'

'But overdressed?'

'Not necessarily. I've yet to meet the man who doesn't look better dressed in a shirt and tie.'

'Hmm. I see.' Half turning towards her, he said, 'The box on the back seat is for you.'

It was a lightweight cardboard box of the size that she'd often seen an orchid presented in and she thought that, if it was, it would look better on him than her. A rare bloom was not meant to be worn on a baggy white sweater!

It wasn't an orchid. Inside the box was an Easter egg with her name piped across it in white icing. It lay on a bed of silk flowers and had a bow of golden ribbon on top. Expensive, obviously chosen with care, it was a prize example of its kind.

'Lucas, it's lovely,' she said laughingly. 'I can't remember when last I had an Easter egg. I shall treasure it.'

'Don't get carried away. It's for eating—not keeping,' he said with a sideways glance at her face and, because he seemed to be telling her not to read too much into the gesture, she turned away and stared through the window.

'What's the matter now?' he wanted to know.

'Did Marina like hers?'

'Don't be ridiculous.'

'Is that a "yes" or a "no"?'

'Neither.'

'So you haven't bought an Easter egg for the woman you're committed to?'

Claudia couldn't believe she was making such an issue of a trivial thing, but it was as if some demon were driving her on.

'Yes, I *have* bought an Easter egg for the woman I'm committed to. Does that satisfy you?'

Of course it didn't. The only thing that would satisfy

her was to be told that the sultry widow was out of his life, and he'd just put paid to any hopes on that score.

'Did you have a nice day with her yesterday?'

'What?'

'You said that you were spending Good Friday with the Beauchamps.'

'Yes, it was very pleasant, except for the fact that young Peter wasn't feeling very well due to the chemotherapy.'

Claudia was immediately ashamed. She was niggling away about Marina, not giving a thought to the boy, when both mother and son had a huge worry on their hands.

But Lucas hadn't forgotten. He was there for them when they needed him and had given up a day of his holiday to be with them.

Yet shouldn't that be where he wanted to be now? He'd admitted that he'd made a commitment to Marina and he wasn't the type to be coaxed into doing something he didn't want.

So why didn't she stop fretting and make the most of this time that he was spending with *her*? It had been *his* suggestion that they had this outing so he obviously wasn't here on sufferance.

'I'm sorry to hear that Peter isn't well,' she said contritely. 'It's so easy to forget that the children we treat in Lizzie's don't always leave us in good health. You do think he's going to be all right, don't you?'

'One can never be sure with cancer,' he said, 'but, yes, I do think he stands a good chance. At one time I would have had to consider amputation, but with new treatments coming out all the time I hope that it won't come to that.

'But we're not here to talk shop, Claudia. I shall be keeping a very close watch on Peter's progress. So let's leave it at that, shall we?'

She nodded. He was right and *she* was to blame for putting a blight on the morning.

'So what shall we talk about?' she asked.

'How about telling me what kind of people your parents are?'

'My mother is fair-skinned like myself. We look very much alike but she is smaller than I am…and my father is a shrewd businessman, but kind and loving with Mum and I. Their best friends are Jack's parents who live nearby.'

Lucas took his gaze off the road for a second and eyed her blankly. 'You mean to say he lived near you?'

'Yes. Why? Does it matter?'

'Er…no. It's just that I imagined he was someone you'd met at college.'

'We grew up together,' she told him steadily. 'As I've told you before, he was the only man I've ever had a relationship with.'

'Did you sleep together?'

She would have told anyone else to mind their own business, but not this man. It was important that he should know all there was to know about her.

'Yes, we slept together, but we didn't make love. He was too ill. It was for comfort rather than sex. I still have my virginity.'

It wasn't a boast, or something to be ashamed about as some of the women she'd known felt it to be, but a simple statement of fact, and as silence fell between them she wondered what comment it would bring forth.

'So we *do* have something in common,' he said casually, in the sort of tone she might expect him to use while discussing the weather, or what they should have for lunch.

Claudia turned in her seat. He'd never slept with a woman! Was that what he was saying? This mesmeric, fascinating member of the opposite sex, who could have any woman he wanted without lifting a finger, had never taken one of them to his bed?

Had he been so bogged down with family and career that he'd never found the time? Surely not! Or was it because he was choosy, and thought that the woman good enough for him hadn't been created? Or maybe he'd been waiting for 'Miss Right' and she'd finally come along in the form of 'Mrs Right'.

'You never cease to amaze me!' she croaked as their glances locked.

He was smiling. 'You haven't seen anything yet,' and, as a signpost loomed up in front of them, 'You'd better start directing me. We're almost there.'

'God! After the bustle of Lizzie's and the never-ending grind of London's traffic, I feel as if I've died and gone to heaven,' Lucas said as they stood in the garden in the spring dusk. 'It's so quiet here, Claudia. I could stay for ever.'

'Yes, it is lovely,' she agreed, 'but I don't think the adrenaline would flow fast enough for you here. You'd miss the challenge that working at Lizzie's presents, and London's special magic that is always there in spite of its teeming masses and endless traffic.'

He laughed. 'So speaks the voice of reason, but it would be nice to have a second home in a place like this, near enough to elegant Cheltenham and yet far enough away to find peace. I suppose I could have words with my bank manager. It would make a change from my prison cell.'

It was Claudia's turn to laugh. 'Your apartment on the hospital complex is very nice.'

'It'll do for the time being, I suppose,' he said dismissively. 'I've never cared where I lived before.'

'And now you do?'

'Maybe. If you remember, I did say that I was contemplating changing my lifestyle.'

Don't take him up on that she warned herself. You'll only spoil the frail harmony between you.

'I can see why this man attracts you,' her mother said in a low voice as they cleared away after the meal. 'He would attract me if I were your age.'

'I'm glad you're not, then,' Claudia said wryly. 'I've got enough competition with the widow of a friend of his.'

'But the thing is,' her mother went on, 'how does *he* feel about *you*?'

'I wish I knew.'

'He watches you all the time, if that's anything to go by.'

'That's because he doesn't like to miss anything.'

'Does he know about Jack?'

'Yes, and he understands, I think.'

'Is the pain any less?'

'Yes. Meeting Lucas Morrison has made it go away and I feel disloyal, though God knows why as Lucas has barely touched me.'

'Jack would want you to be happy,' her mother said gently. 'He wouldn't want you to continue carrying his cross for him.'

'I know,' she said quietly, and went to sit beside the man who had brought her out of darkness, into a better kind of light.

CHAPTER SEVEN

THE chill of a spring evening was all around them as Claudia and Lucas walked home from the quaint village pub that had been full of local people and a smattering of early tourists.

They'd sat beside a log fire in a huge iron grate and talked of this and that. Her parents. His sister and little Craig. Oliver, the trendy student. London theatres. Everything except Marina Beauchap...and Jack Tomlin.

In a moment that wasn't without embarrassment Claudia had been obliged to introduce Lucas to Jack's parents when they'd called unexpectedly after dinner and had met the question in their eyes with a calmness that she was far from feeling.

How Lucas had seen the meeting was hard to tell. She had prayed that he wasn't thinking they'd been tipped off and had come to view their son's replacement, because it certainly wasn't so.

For one thing she would never be party to anything so distasteful, and for another he'd given her no cause to think it was a role he would be willing to step into.

He had acted with restrained pleasantness. The Tomlins had been their usual friendly selves and her parents had behaved accordingly. It had seemed to Claudia that she was the only one who was uncomfortable.

And now, as they walked home down the deserted main street of the village, she was surprised when he took her hand in his.

It was weeks since they'd had any degree of physical

contact. The last time had been on the corridor outside the orthopaedic wards and that seemed a lifetime ago.

'What are you thinking, Claudia?' he asked as they strolled along. 'We've talked about a lot of things while we were in the pub and I don't believe one of them was what was really in your mind. To begin with, you haven't asked me what I thought about the appearance of the Tomlins. Whether I felt intimidated.'

She'd been solemn before but that brought a smile. 'Intimidated is a word that I would never associate with you. Annoyed, taken aback, irritated, maybe, but never that.'

'All right, then, one of those things, because I could see that you were most uncomfortable during their visit.'

'What would you have expected?' she asked. 'If you must know, I was totally embarrassed on your behalf. I should have anticipated that they might drop by and warned you of the possibility. But, Lucas, what does it matter? As long as you weren't annoyed at being put in such a situation.'

'Why should I be? They are entitled to make what they will of my presence. I certainly meant them no hurt.'

Claudia turned to face him and, with their fingers still entwined, she said huskily, 'I know you didn't. The only person hurting is me.'

His face was bleak in the light of the street lamps and when he spoke the reason for it was there. 'So you are still bound by your grief? You are prepared to be with me, yet hold yourself apart all the time. I suggested this break so that I could get to know you better, but you are an enigma, Claudia.'

'And I suppose you aren't!' she exclaimed, her voice rising. 'When I said I was hurting you jumped to your own conclusions as usual. I'm not still ''bound by grief'' as you describe it, but there are other things that can cause misery besides grief.'

'Such as?'

'The complexities of another person's mind.'

'Am I being taken to task because there are moments when I can't resist you, such as now, with your eyes sparkling fire, your mouth sweet and vulnerable, and the rest of you wanting it as much as I do?'

'Wanting what?' she snapped angrily.

'This, of course…as if you didn't know,' and, releasing her hand, he took her in his arms so forcibly that her feet were barely touching the pavement beneath them.

Claudia gave a sighing sort of moan as their mouths connected and then gave herself up to the desire that was never far away when she was with him.

Their thick jackets were blunting body contact and without moving her lips from his she quickly unzipped hers and guided his hands inside it, so that he might feel the fast beating of her heart and the taut, tilting breasts that had their own message for him.

'These are games that lovers play, Claudia,' Lucas said at last. 'We must be mad.'

She stiffened in his arms. At times like this they *were* lovers…as far as she was concerned, anyway. Everything else receded…Jack…Marina Beauchamp…the fact that Lucas was the shining light of Orthopaedics at a famous hospital and she was on a far lower rung of the ladder. Nothing mattered, except that she was in his arms.

But if his last remark was anything to go by she was the only one who saw it that way and, hating herself for being so malleable and suppliant, she whizzed up the zip of her jacket with an angry flourish and pointed herself towards home, leaving Lucas to lengthen his stride to keep level.

Her parents were in bed when they got back to the house and, not giving him the chance to use his chemistry-cum-caution on her another time, she said curtly, 'If you want a drink you know where the kitchen is.'

With one foot on the bottom stair and the same chill in her voice she went on, 'What time do you want us to leave in the morning?'

He shrugged. 'Whatever I say won't be right, so I'll leave it to you.'

'Mid-morning, then?'

'OK…and, Claudia…'

'Yes?'

'I know what you think of me.'

'You don't!' she flared back. 'If you did you wouldn't be such a patronising beast.'

'Why do I always feel that is how you see me…as some sort of animal?'

She was halfway up the stairs by this time and, looking down on him frostily, she put thoughts into words. 'That is exactly how I do see you. To me you're the "urban tiger",' and, as his eyes widened, 'So there you are!'

After her angry departure Lucas seated himself in the darkened lounge. He didn't want a drink, or anything else for that matter, except perhaps for one thing and he'd just foolishly let it slip out of reach.

His face was sombre but there was grim amusement inside him. The 'urban tiger'! So that was how his young assistant saw him. As a powerful beast, living in an unnatural habitat.

She was crazy! Yet, like the magnificent animal she'd likened him to, he'd had to fight for survival too. But he was tamed now. Love had tamed him. Love for his family, the children in his care, and for a woman who, though she wouldn't admit it, needed him just as much, or even more, than they did.

Talk between them over Sunday breakfast was friendly enough as neither of them wanted Claudia's parents to pick up on any aggravation. As her father held her in the last few seconds before she got into the car he said in a low voice, 'Your mother and I approve of this man, darling daughter. Hold onto him.'

She sighed. 'It would be easier to contain an eel, Dad.'

He laughed. 'Yes, but how much more credit is due to the one who catches the slippery creature, than the captor of the languorous toad.'

Claudia was laughing as the car moved away and Lucas said brusquely, 'It's good to see that something can make you smile. What's the joke?'

'We were having a conversation about an eel and a toad,' she told him blandly, wondering how amused he would be to find that the tiger was now being likened to a wriggling eel.

As the car ate up the miles, he said into the silence that had fallen between them, 'While you were sharing your little joke with your father, your mother was telling me that you're thinking of changing apartments. Why didn't you tell me?'

'I didn't think you'd be interested.'

'Why not let me be the judge of that? Where are you thinking of moving to?'

Claudia could tell by his voice that he was irritated and she wondered why. Maybe he thought she was contemplating moving next to door to him.

'I was walking down Harley Street the other day,' she explained calmly, 'and saw a roof-top apartment advertised in one of those delightful tall houses that are split into private consulting suites. This one was occupied by dentists on all three floors with the vacant apartment up above and, as it was so much nearer to Lizzie's than where I am now, I thought I might view it.'

'Are you mad?' he spluttered. 'Contemplating living over the top of some mausoleum where you will be the only person in the building during the night!'

'I don't know why you're getting so steamed up about it,' she countered back. 'Haven't you heard of burglar alarms and locks and bolts?'

'Yes, I have,' he replied grimly, 'and I've also heard of lunatics who don't see those sort of things as a deterrent. If you're determined to view it I'm coming with you!'

'All right, then! Do so! Although I *am* old enough to take care of myself.'

'That's debatable.'

'Huh! Although maybe you're right. I don't seem to show much sense when you're around.'

'If you're referring to last night, forget it. I have,' he informed her dourly.

'Oh! So that's how little it meant to you. I told you once that I didn't ever want you to touch me again and I meant it. Last night you took me unawares.'

He was laughing at her now. 'Really? I noticed that the reluctant virgin was conspicuous by her absence.'

Claudia felt her face flame. 'That is the last thing I will ever tell you if I'm going to keep getting it thrown back in my face.'

He became serious. 'I'm sorry, Claudia. You were right to call me a beast, but promise that you will let me view the apartment with you.'

'Yes, all right,' she agreed, wishing that their viewing it together meant something other than his concern for her safety.

They were back in London by the middle of the afternoon and when he stopped the Rover in front of her place Claudia invited him in for a coffee.

Lucas shook his head. 'No, thanks just the same. I want to call on Sophie and the baby. She's been on the phone a couple of times recently and I think that she's finding Dimitri heavy going. I warned her about the age gap and the nationality difference, but would she listen?'

Was it an excuse that he'd just come up with to bring the turbulent weekend to an end? she wondered as he drove away. Or was his sister really unhappy with 'Dimmy'?

Monday morning brought a florist's delivery man onto the orthopaedic wards with a huge bouquet of flowers for Dr Claudia Craven.

As the staff gathered around to share the moment and observe her surprise, she thought tremulously that Lucas hadn't meant what he'd said about those precious moments on the deserted pavement of the main street of the village and this was his way of showing it.

When she read the card that was attached her face changed. The sender was Faisal Al Saud. She might have known that Lucas wouldn't go back on what he'd said. The card said:

> May we meet some time, Dr Craven? I admire beautiful women and you are one. Please get in touch. Faisal Al Saud.'

'Whew! You've made a conquest there,' Robin said, voicing the thoughts of all those present.

'I'm not very happy about that,' she said vexedly. 'He's not my type.'

'He likes you, though,' Jess Richardson teased, and Claudia thought that it was typical of life that the man she wanted kept her guessing all the time, while Faisal was obviously interested in her. Why hadn't he gone back to Kuwait with the rest of the family? Surely it wasn't because of her?

Her determination to view the roof-top flat had strengthened after the conversation in the car with Lucas the day before and, knowing that most estate agents were keyed in to the fact that Easter was the time when some of the population had itchy feet, Claudia rang the number on the board outside the property to see if she might view later in the day.

It was in the lunch-hour when she made the call and, just as she had expected, they were open for business and only too willing to let her look over the premises.

So far there had been no sign of Lucas on the wards, which meant there had been no opportunity to ask if he would be available to go with her late that afternoon, but as she was leaving the restaurant on the end of her lunch-hour he was coming towards her with Marina Beauchamp by his side.

If she could have avoided them she would—mainly because she was carrying the huge bouquet from Faisal Al Saud in her arms, intending passing it onto one of the other wards where she wouldn't have to look at it.

They were deep in conversation but when he saw her Lucas excused himself and left his companion to carry on alone.

'I've been in a resources meeting,' he explained, with a question in his eyes as he observed the flowers. 'Any problems on the unit?'

Claudia shook her head, wishing she'd managed to pass on the blooms before she'd met Lucas.

'No, not really. There are two new admissions. One is the girl with scoliosis that you have brought in for surgery, and the other is an accident victim that Miles Soper has operated on.'

He nodded. 'Not bad, considering we're on the tail-end of a holiday weekend.' Turning his attention to the flowers, he asked, 'So what's with the mobile garden?'

He bent over to read the card attached to them and his face darkened, 'So the Sheikh of Araby hasn't given up on you?'

'So it would seem,' she admitted, wishing Faisal Al Saud back in his native land with all speed.

'And are you going to take him up on his request?'

'I thought that we'd already decided that I'm not cut out for the harem. Of course I'm not going to meet him. I'm on my way to deposit these in one of the other wards. I'm going to take *you* up on your offer, though.'

For a brief moment she had the satisfaction of seeing him lost for words and then he said slowly, 'What offer?'

Claudia laughed. 'You have a very short memory.'

Still not tuned in, he said shortly, 'Not true.'

'I've made an appointment to view for four-thirty this afternoon.'

His brow cleared. 'Oh, that offer. And you want to know if I'm coming? The answer is yes. We'll walk there. It's only a matter of minutes from here.'

'Er…right, then. I wasn't sure if you'd still want to come.'

'Well, now you know. Somebody has to keep an eye on you, what with roof-top apartments being under consideration and predatory Arabs hanging around.'

She eyed him levelly. 'I'm quite capable of looking after

myself. I did travel around the world with a very sick man…and managed to avoid coming to any harm. Just because you have to be a guardian angel to your family and the Beauchamps all the time, you don't have to add me to the list of dependants with a capital ''D''.'

'I'll bear that in mind,' he said drily, 'and now I'm going to eat…while you get rid of the floral enticement.'

Ten-year-old Hannah Horrocks who had been admitted that morning had seen Lucas in his clinic some months previously. Her parents had brought her to him on the recommendation of their GP because of the girl's worsening posture.

A change in the shape of the child's spine had become evident with some poor posturing of the shoulder and the pelvic area. X-rays had shown adolescent scoliosis to be the cause.

Claudia had seen from the patient's notes that Lucas had been faced with either subjecting Hannah to long-term corrective treatment, covering a period of years, or operating on the spine.

His decision to carry out spinal fusion was because it would be less traumatic for the child than years of plaster casts and bracing, and also because the depth of the thoracic curve of the spine and the fact that there was lordosis—inward curving—present made the problem too serious to rely on slower methods.

When she was taken down to surgery he would expose the affected vertebrae and perform joint fusion along with a bone graft made up of bone chips from the pelvis.

Hannah would then have to endure bedrest for a few weeks and the discomfort of a plaster cast for six months until full fusion of the spine had been achieved.

All very distressing for a young girl, but in later years

she would be glad of the straight spine that had been the gift of St Elizabeth's orthopaedic unit.

The agents had let Claudia have the key on the promise that she would bring it back before five-thirty and as they let themselves into the elegant old building Claudia looked around her with wide-eyed interest.

The first thing she noticed was the silence. There was only the sound of their footsteps on the marble floor of the main entrance hall and it became clear that the dentists who had their private practices on the premises were either on holiday or had finished for the day.

Lucas was looking around him, keen dark eyes taking in every detail of this example of Harley Street health care.

'Very impressive!' he commented. 'And how tranquil. It's hard to believe that the bustle of London is only a few feet away.'

He was right there, she thought. It was so quiet in this place, it was scary.

A fine curving staircase wound its way from floor to floor and, rejecting the speedier transportation of the lift, they climbed it together, with Lucas all the time expressing approval of the surroundings.

As the door swung back to let them into the apartment the first thing she saw was an endless army of chimney pots of all shapes and sizes standing proud on a thousand roofs, and instead of rapturising at the sight Claudia was assailed with a feeling of loneliness.

He was right. Alone at night in this place she would feel isolated. Supposing a shadowy figure with a balaclava on its head came slinking across the roof-tops to where she was sleeping, or the place set on fire?

The apartment itself was tastefully furnished with expensive curtains and a new fitted kitchen and modern bathroom, but she knew immediately that they wouldn't make up for the feeling of being alone on top of the world. Solitude was one thing. Isolation was another.

It seemed that Lucas wasn't seeing it in the same light, though. He appeared to be impressed with the whole thing and kept exclaiming how cosy and private she would be in the roof-top flat.

It was galling to have to admit that he'd been right about the place not being suitable, but she had to stop him before he became any more entranced with it and so she told him reluctantly, 'If you like it so much, why don't you have it?'

'Don't tell me you're not interested!' he said with over-done surprise. 'This place has so many advantages.'

'Such as?'

'You could study bird life. That's where you find them—on the roof-tops. And if the lift is full or broken down, just think of all the exercise you'll get running up and down those stairs. Not to mention how convenient it will be if you discover that you need a filling or a tooth crowned.'

He was laughing openly, eyes bright with amusement. 'Of course you don't want this place. It's a classy apartment with lots of atmosphere for a couple, maybe, or even a family with grown-up kids, but not a beautiful woman on her own.'

Holding out his hand, he said, 'Let's go. I'll race you down the stairs.' Forgetting her chagrin at being laughed at, she picked up her long skirt and set off.

They reached the ground floor together and as they collapsed onto a seat in the foyer Lucas said, 'I've seen funeral parlours with more life in them than this place. Only one thing remains before we return to Lizzie's.'

'What's that?'

'You admit that the urban tiger knows best when it comes to choosing a lair.'

Claudia groaned. 'I suppose I'll never hear the last of that. I don't know what possessed me to tell you.'

'I'm waiting,' he said.

'I admit that you were right, but I am disappointed. I've always wanted to be on Harley Street and this seemed about the only way I'm ever likely to achieve it.'

He was getting to his feet, serious now. 'You never know what the future holds, Claudia. I hope that yours will hold only good things. When I try to look into mine it always seems to be foggy.' Taking her hand, he led her out into the noisy outside world.

Walking back to the hospital, Claudia had mixed feelings. It was comforting to know that he cared about her welfare. Not quite so satisfying to know that he'd been right and she'd been wrong about the Harley Street flat. Even less reassuring was the knowledge that he didn't see his future very clearly and that was coming from one of the most decisive men she'd ever known.

'How were Sophie and the baby when you called yesterday?' she asked as they approached Cavendish Square with the bright lights of Oxford Street beyond.

It was a deliberate change of subject, yet she did want to know. Anything connected with Lucas Morrison was of interest to her.

'All right,' he said absently as if his mind was elsewhere. 'Dimitri is thinking of selling the restaurant and taking them to live in Greece.'

'Oh! You'll miss them if he does that, won't you?'

'Yes, but I have to admit that life would be simpler. Sometimes I think I'm too available for Sophie and Oliver, but there's the baby. I don't want to miss seeing young Craig growing up.'

'Maybe you should start a family of your own...or take on a ready-made one.'

'I'd prefer to have a wife first. An essential ingredient, don't you think?'

'You need a woman to give you children, yes, but not necessarily a wife. Lots of couples dispense with the formalities these days.'

'And you agree with that?'

'Not entirely. It's everyone to their own choice. Personally I would want my children to be born within a marriage.'

Lizzie's was looming up ahead and as they prepared to separate, he to his utilitarian flatlet and she to the underground car park where the Boxter was waiting, Lucas said as if she hadn't spoken, 'I hope you won't regret not going after the apartment on Harley Street. Thinking about it now I feel that I didn't let you make up your own mind.'

She smiled. 'I'd made up my mind the moment I walked into the place. It was too quiet...and, Lucas...?'

'Yes?'

'Thanks for coming with me. It was on a crazy impulse that I decided to view.'

He nodded. 'We all have crazy impulses.'

'Like Saturday night?'

'Yes. I'd say that was a good example.' Without giving her time to rally from that dampener, he went.

As Claudia went down to the car park a helicopter roared overhead, bound for the heli-pad on the hospital roof, either about to deliver a seriously ill patient or to pick one up.

In an emergency, or in a remote area, there was nothing

to equal them for speed and accessibility. Countless lives had been saved by using the air services for the seriously ill or injured and today would be no different. A team of doctors and nurses would have been notified beforehand of its arrival and would be waiting to take over.

As she bent to get into the car a figure came out of the shadows and as alarm bells rang Claudia thrust herself into the seat and locked the door.

'There is no need to be afraid, Dr Craven,' a smooth voice with foreign intonations said beside the locked window. 'I happened to see you arriving. Did you receive the flowers?'

'What are you doing here?' she asked.

'I came to see you.'

'I thought you would have been back in your own country by now.'

She wound down the window and smiled up at him, thanking him politely for the flowers.

It was at that precise moment when she was looking up at him that she saw Lucas striding swiftly towards them.

'What's going on here?' he asked.

'I was just thanking Mr Al Saud for his flowers.'

'I see,' he said grimly as Faisal gave a stiff little bow and departed.

'You weren't exactly giving him the cold shoulder,' he said accusingly. 'I thought you didn't like the fellow? And how do you come to be meeting him in here?'

Relief at being free of Faisal's attentions was wiped out by annoyance. 'He was parking his car and saw me arrive...in case you think it was pre-arranged,' she snapped. 'As to my being friendly towards him, it seemed the best way to handle what might develop into a tricky situation. And what are you doing here?'

'Does it matter?'

'Yes, it does. You are demanding to know why Faisal Al Saud was here and I am just as interested to know why you showed up.'

'I was watching from my window, waiting for you to drive out, as there have been one or two incidents down here. When you didn't appear I came to see why…and what do I find? That your non-appearance is because you're having a cosy little chat with Omar's son!'

'There was nothing cosy about it,' she said quietly as her anger drained away. 'I was scared stiff that I was going to be bundled into his limo and transported to a warmer climate. Your appearance certainly solved my problem and I thank you for your concern, but your doubts about my intentions rather take the edge off it, I'm afraid.'

He was about to reply but Claudia didn't give him the chance. As the car moved forward she saluted him briefly and was gone.

That night, alone in her apartment, Claudia thought how wonderful it would have been if they'd been viewing the roof-top flat for them to share.

A love-nest beneath the stars that they could share in happy solitude. But it was clear that had been the furthest thing from the mind of the mystery that was Lucas Morrison. He'd been concerned for her, given up his precious time to look it over, but it had ended there.

His interest in her welfare had also been in evidence when he'd come striding into the car park and sent Faisal packing, but she knew he would be just as protective over any woman in those circumstances. So there was no point in reading anything into the two happenings.

It was the other guidelines that he was so fond of handing out that she should be following, such as the fact that he saw his future as not clearly defined.

She supposed she ought to feel the same, but if he would only say the word her future would be crystal clear: a pathway beside the man who had brought her back to life.

As she slipped between smooth satin sheets Claudia turned her head and tried to imagine how it would feel to see his head beside her on the pillow, feel his arms around her, and to experience the magic of relinquishing her virginity in ecstatic union.

The depth of her sigh as she turned back to gaze up at the ceiling was an indication of how far away that scenario was. Snuggling beneath the covers, she asked herself if a passionate Arab could be a substitute for a supposedly cold-blooded Englishman and knew the answer to be 'no'.

CHAPTER EIGHT

HANNAH HORROCKS was first on the list for surgery the following morning and Lucas eyed Claudia thoughtfully over his blue theatre pyjamas when she arrived to assist him.

'And how are you this morning, Dr Craven?' he asked. 'Raring to go?'

She *was* raring to go but wasn't quite sure as to where. It was a bright, clear morning with spring definitely in the air and for once the pull that she always felt from Lizzie's hadn't been there as she'd driven towards Regent's Park.

There had been a yearning inside her to be out in the open, watching the world come to life beneath spring sunshine, with Lucas beside her, his dark, arresting charm centred entirely on herself.

But, instead, a sick little girl needed help, as did others, and the golden spring would have to unfold itself without her, for today anyway.

'Yes, I'm raring to go, Dr Morrison,' she told him, 'but I have to admit that it wasn't exactly in this direction that I was drawn as I drove in this morning. Spring creates a sort of restlessness inside us, don't you think?'

He was smiling his sardonic smile. 'There are lots of things to make us restless, that eat away at our content, Claudia, and I suppose this time of year is one of them. Although with the kind of life I live I barely have time to take note of the seasons coming and going. If I'm not fully occupied here at St Elizabeth's, I'm at a conference, or lecturing somewhere, and then there's...'

'Your relatives?'

'Yes, my family ties, and...'

He paused and she butted in, 'The Beauchamps?'

'I suppose so.'

Irritation rose in her. What did he mean? He supposed so? Either he was involved with Marina Beauchamp...or he wasn't! Where was his normal decisiveness?

She turned away and began to scrub up, her face set and angry. Keep your mind entirely on the job, she told herself, and for goodness' sake stop wishing for the moon. Lucas Morrison is just as far out of your sights as that great golden ball in the sky.

And keep her mind on the job she did as Lucas began the tricky operation that would hopefully give a straight spine to a worried child who was approaching adolescence.

After the unnerving meeting with Faisal Al Saud in the car park Claudia was hoping she'd seen the last of him and she was totally dismayed when he appeared in the restaurant at lunch-time and came to stand by her table.

'Good morning, Dr Craven,' he said in his precise English. 'I hope you are well?'

'Yes, thank you, Mr Al Saud,' she replied coolly. 'What can I do for you?'

'There are many things you could do for me, but sadly you choose not to do them,' he rejoined. 'So today I fly back to Kuwait. That is all I came to tell you.' Before she'd had time to take in what he was saying he was bowing in a similar fashion to the night before and bidding her farewell, a tall, dark-skinned figure in a cream suit that stood out starkly amongst the more conservative wear of the other diners.

As he was leaving the restaurant he came face to face

with Lucas and, watching the two men acknowledge each other with cold politeness, Claudia felt her heart sink.

Not without cause, it seemed, as Lucas came striding across to her table. 'So he's still hanging around?' he said brusquely. 'Most men will take no for an answer. The fact that he doesn't makes me think that you are egging him on.'

'Egging him on!' she shrieked in a voice that made heads turn. 'How dare you? And even if I were, what has it got to do with you?'

'Maybe not a lot,' he admitted with a dour smile, 'but I am in part responsible for my staff.'

'Rubbish!' she cried, still with a volume that was directing attention towards them. 'You are only responsible for my behaviour when I'm in theatre or on the wards. What I do the rest of the time is not your business. So when next you see me with Omar's son just remember that, will you?'

The tiger was poised. She could almost feel his claws. 'So you *are* going to start a relationship with him?'

Claudia was calm now that she'd got him rattled. 'Maybe. It's early days, but the man does have lots of charm.'

'You're insane,' he hissed.

She got to her feet. 'Past tense. I have been, but my sanity has just returned. Bye, Lucas. Enjoy your meal.'

'You'll regret this, madam,' he said through clenched teeth as she began to move away.

'Bye-ee,' she called sweetly over her shoulder.

The moment she was out of sight Claudia knew she'd behaved like an idiot. She was jealous of Lucas and Marina Beauchamp and so she'd created a stupid fantasy about

herself and Faisal which was going to be impossible to
follow through.

When Lucas became aware of that he would see just
how pathetic she was and it was a daunting thought. In the
meantime she would have to keep up the silly charade for
as long as she could and endure the consequences when
the time came.

'You look somewhat ruffled,' Robin said when she went
back to the ward.

'That's exactly what I am,' she admitted. 'Lucas thinks
there's something going on between Faisal Al Saud and
myself.'

Her young counterpart eyed her sympathetically. 'And
because you have feelings for our revered bone-
straightener you are not happy?'

'So you've guessed that I'm in love with him?' she
questioned dismally.

'We've all noticed that you gravitate towards each other
at every opportunity, if that's what you mean. So what's
the problem?'

'Marina Beauchamp, the glamorous social worker. She
comes first with Lucas.'

Robin eyed her in surprise. 'You're kidding! The over-
blown widow is way behind you in the beauty stakes.'

'My beauty only seems to appeal to men from a warmer
climate.'

'The Arab?'

'Yes.'

'And are you seeing him?'

'No, of course not. He's flying back to Kuwait today.'

'Does Lucas know that?'

'No, and I don't want him to find out. Promise?'

'Yes, if that's what you want,' Robin agreed reluctantly,

and as two of the nurses came into view the conversation came to an end.

In the weeks after that there was cold politeness between herself and Lucas. Claudia was tempted a few times to tell him that Faisal wasn't even in the country, but pride and the fact that Marina seemed to be always hovering around him made her hold back.

Robin had started dating Carolyn, one of the nurses on the neurology unit, and Claudia invited them round one night for supper.

It was pleasant to have the company and the opportunity to try some serious cooking for once, but as she saw how engrossed they were in each other her longing for contact with Lucas was like a sick hunger that the tasty meal she'd served wasn't going to appease.

When they'd gone, with arms entwined, so close they seemed as if they were joined at the hip, she felt restless and on edge. Obeying an impulse that she knew to be anything but sensible, she got out the Boxter and pointed it towards the apartment block beside Lizzie's where Lucas lived.

What she was going to do when she got there, she had no idea, but the desire to be in the vicinity was too strong to ignore. If he came out and saw the Boxter she would want to curl up and die, but it was a risk she had to take if she wanted to be near him.

His curtains were open and incredibly she could see him pacing the room with the same sort of restlessness as the beast she had likened him to.

Was it the balmy spring night that was making them both like this? she wondered. It was too much to hope that he was as desperate to see her as she was to be with him.

He disappeared from sight suddenly and when he appeared seconds later he was wearing an outdoor jacket. Claudia went rigid. Any moment he would be out on the forecourt of the flats and he would see her car.

As she drove off, aware that it was the fastest departure she'd ever made, there was some peace in her. Not a lot, but at least she'd seen him.

She would be seeing him again tomorrow on the wards and for many months to come, but that was in public. Tonight she'd wanted to be near him away from bone deformities and plaster casts. It was too bad that she'd only been able to do that by skulking outside his apartment.

As he saw the tail-lights of the Boxter disappearing Lucas stopped in his tracks. It couldn't be Claudia at this time of night. She would be tucked up in her flat, or out with the latest man in her life.

His face was bleak as he went through a side door that would lead him up to the wards. One of his small patients was causing him anxiety to the extent that he was making a late-night visit to the unit.

After he'd satisfied himself that at last a healing process was underway, Lucas walked slowly back home, and as he stripped for bed a vision of smooth golden skin, tempting thighs and high, thrusting breasts caused him to observe his own nakedness with a rueful eye.

When they were doing the ward rounds together the next morning Lucas said coolly, 'There was a Boxter outside the hospital late last night.'

'Really?'

'Yes. Was it yours? I didn't manage to get the number.'

'Why would it be mine?' she countered. 'I was entertaining at my apartment last night.'

He was eyeing her with eyes like flint. 'Bedding the Bedouin, were you?'

'If you choose to think so.'

'Is there an alternative?'

'Yes. Quite a few, as a matter of fact, but I don't see why I should spell them out, as you are determined to jump to your own conclusions.'

Claudia was hurt and very angry but there was no way he was going to see it. What was the matter with the man? The rest of the staff could see how she felt about him, so why couldn't he?

She could tell him that she loved him, of course, but if a woman did that and the man responded she would never know if he would have done so in any case, or if he was capitulating because the offer was being put in front of him on a plate.

After that cold exchange of words the day became like many others over past weeks and by the time Claudia had done her hours and was ready to leave for home she was seriously thinking of moving to another hospital.

'You can't do that!' Robin exclaimed the next morning when she told him what she was contemplating. 'I just can't imagine what Lucas would be like if you went.'

'He would be just the same as he is now,' she told him flatly. 'Cold, efficient, censorious, quick to judge. I could go on for ever.'

'So you don't think he'd miss you?'

'Only in the sense that he would have no one to demoralise repeatedly.'

'You really are fed up, aren't you?'

'Yes, I am, to such an extent that I'm going to leave in a month's time, even if I haven't found myself a situation elsewhere.'

The moment she'd said it Claudia knew it was the sensible thing to do. Coming back to Lizzie's had been a mistake. Not from any fault of the famous hospital, but because she'd met Lucas here and been captivated from the moment he'd erupted into the lift that first morning of her return.

She would have to tell him, of course, but the procedure was that first she must notify the clinical tutor who dealt with training for junior doctors and staffing levels, and then the details of her departure would go to Personnel, but after yesterday's cold exchange between Lucas and herself she was in no hurry to be the recipient of further barbed comments.

Anger came flooding back at the memory of it. He'd accused her of 'bedding the Bedouin!' What a nerve! And what a pity she hadn't come back with a knife thrust of her own such as, 'seducing the social worker,' or 'wooing the widow.'

If she had been intending telling him of her decision the opportunity would have been denied her. Leaving Robin to make what he would of her future plans, she went to talk to Sheila Newcome, who was a much less difficult person these days, and was told, 'Lucas won't be in today. His secretary says that he's taking time off to deal with some personal business.'

Immediately dread took over. It would be just like him to get married quickly and without fuss, but when she made an excuse to visit the social workers' office Marina was at her desk and not showing any signs of unusual excitement.

Her next port of call was to see Belinda, who eyed her in surprise when she saw Claudia's solemn expression.

'Hi, Claudia. What's wrong?' she questioned.

The girl who had come back to Lizzie's a shadow of

her former self had been looking much happier of late and Belinda had a suspicion that it was something to do with a certain orthopaedic consultant, but this morning there was no glow about her and her friend was anxious to know why.

'I'm leaving,' Claudia told her. 'I've passed on the information to the right departments and was about to inform Lucas, but I believe he's away on private business.'

Belinda stared at her. 'You're leaving! Why, for goodness' sake?'

Claudia's smile was wry. Belinda wouldn't let her get away without squeezing the truth out of her, but she was going to play it down for all she was worth.

She was using the excuse that she wanted to tell Lucas of her decision as a means of finding out why he was taking time off...not that it was any of her business.

'Shall we say a conflict of personalities?' she said in answer to the question.

Belinda groaned as the light dawned. 'Not with Lucas?'

''Fraid so.'

'Oh, Claudia!' she wailed. 'I thought that you and he might...'

'No chance. He's got something going with Marina Beauchamp.'

'I know that they're very friendly,' his secretary agreed. 'She absolutely dotes on him, but I don't know if he feels the same.'

'He's told me that he's made a commitment to her,' Claudia said casually as if it were of minor interest, 'which made me wonder if he was taking time off to get married.'

Belinda shook her head in disbelief. 'I don't think so! Surely he would have said. But let's get back to you, Claudy. Where are you going? You're not leaving medicine, surely?'

'No, of course not. I'm going to take a break and then go abroad,' she said on the spur of the moment. 'Somewhere in the Third World where the need for medical staff is the greatest.'

'Not to India, then?'

Claudia shook her head. 'No. That place has too many painful memories.'

On leaving Belinda's office she made her way back to the ward and when she told them of her plans there were dismayed exclamations from the staff.

It was comforting to know that they'd be sorry to see her go, especially after the chilly reception she'd received when she'd come back after her long absence.

When Lucas returned from wherever he'd gone there would be no need to tell him personally. Her impending departure would be common knowledge in their part of the hospital.

He was away for three days and during that time Claudia's resolve hardened. It was dreadful without him and would be even more so if she were never to see him again, but there was no use languishing over the unobtainable, she kept telling herself.

Miles Soper was doing the surgery during Lucas's absence with Robin and herself to assist, and every moment she was in theatre Claudia was aware of how much more she enjoyed working with Lucas.

But he wasn't the only orthopaedic wizard in the world, she reasoned. There were plenty as skilled as he, but sadly they wouldn't have his looks and personality, even though it was that same personality that was the root of the trouble between them—as well as his relationship with an attractive widow.

*   *   *

Lucas hadn't been in his office five minutes on the morning of his return when he sent for her. She came across Belinda on the way there and her friend said ruefully, 'He knows. There was a note from the medical staffing officer in Personnel waiting for him.'

'Fine,' Claudia said with assumed calm. 'The sooner we've spoken, the better.'

'What's this?' he asked harshly when she went in, waving the internal memo in front of her.

'I've no idea,' she responded. 'If you'd stop waving it around I might be able to read what's on it.'

'You're leaving?'

'Yes. In a month's time.'

'Why, for God's sake? Belinda says you told her it's because of a conflict of personalities. Whose?'

'Mine and yours.'

Her eyes were devouring him, taking in every detail of the face that haunted her, and the lean, lithe grace of him. She must be insane to be thinking of cutting him out of her life when she cared so much for him.

'And where are you taking yourself off to, might I ask?' he asked with a steely calm that had replaced the harshness of his greeting.

'I'm going abroad.'

It sounded so definite, yet she hadn't a clue what she intended doing once she'd left Lizzie's.

'Don't tell me. You're going to Kuwait.'

At that moment Claudia decided that the Faisal Al Saud myth had gone on long enough.

'Of course I'm not,' she hissed. 'Omar's son has been back in Kuwait since that day you saw us in the restaurant and I've had no contact with him since, nor do I intend to have any in the future.'

'You're lying, Claudia,' he said with sudden weariness.

'I am not lying. I have never had any sort of a relation-ship with Faisal Al Saud. How many times do I have to tell you? It's because of *you* that I'm leaving Lizzie's. You don't treat me properly. One moment you are all sweetness and light…and the next you are cutting me down to size in the way that only you can do. I don't deserve it and I'm not going to put up with it!'

'So you're not involved with the Arab?'

Claudia raised her eyes heavenwards. 'For the last time…no! But it doesn't make any difference. I'm still leaving. It was a mistake coming back here, but I had no way of knowing that I was going to meet…'

'An urban tiger?'

It was her turn to be weary.

'If you like…yes.'

'Even though it might be willing to be tamed?'

'Don't joke about it, Lucas,' she said quietly. 'If you've finished I'll get back to the wards. I'm needed there.'

'Yes, do that,' he agreed. 'I'll be along later. I've got young Peter Beauchamp coming in for tests and I want to supervise them myself. I'm hoping that there will be good news for the boy and his mother.'

'I hope so too,' she said from the doorway, and she did, fervently, but why was it that they couldn't have a con-versation without Marina's name cropping up?

When she had gone Lucas sat looking at the piece of paper in his hand. Claudia had only been back at St Elizabeth's for a few months and now she was off.

As a doctor he was deeply disappointed. She was hard-working and efficient and would doubtless channel those qualities into her new position, wherever it might be, but she was needed here. Couldn't she see that?

She'd said she was going to work abroad. She was actually leaving the country. For a sickening moment he had thought she'd gone crazy and was throwing in her lot with the undeniably wealthy Arab.

But, surprisingly, she had taken that burden from him by explaining that she had been tormenting him with an imaginary relationship that had never got off the ground, and he supposed he'd deserved it with his unfair accusations.

Relief had washed over him like a cleansing tide when he'd discovered that he'd been wrong, but, sadly, he was not forgiven, and from the sound of it she was not going to be swayed into changing her mind.

He'd often thought of taking *his* skills to the Third World, but there had always been responsibilities at home that had held him back. But now he was more or less free of them. Sophie was married to her temperamental Greek, Oliver was on the right path with his sociology course, and there was no longer the need for frequent visits to the home in Worthing.

There was one responsibility that he hadn't yet been released from, but he was hoping that in the near future Marina and her son would find the security they deserved.

When Belinda came back in the office he was still sitting there, and as she eyed him enquiringly Lucas said sombrely, 'She's going, Belinda. Has definitely made up her mind. One of the best assistants I've had in years is leaving me.'

If his secretary noticed that he saw it as Claudia leaving him, rather than Lizzie's, she made no comment, but she did feel driven to tell him, 'I've tried to persuade Claudia not to go, but she is very determined. She's still very vulnerable after her fiancé's death and needs an anchor rather than a flimsy raft. Lizzie's is the right place for her at this time in her life, not some dangerous war zone, or earthquake-riven land. But there are other hurts inside her besides losing Jack and if you and she don't get on, maybe she is doing the right thing.'

Thank you, Belinda, he thought grimly. You have just made it clear what a pain in the neck I am as far as Claudia Craven is concerned.

Heaving himself up out of the chair, with his customary vigour not in evidence, he said flatly, 'I don't intend to interfere. I've already done enough damage.'

He straightened his shoulders as if to throw off some unseen burden. 'With regard to the day ahead, Belinda, I'm having some tests done on Marina's lad this morning and after that I will be on the wards if you need me for anything.'

When Claudia returned to the ward after the bleak exchange of words with Lucas she could hear laughter and music issuing forth even before she got there.

A young auxiliary nurse was hurrying past carrying a pile of bed linen and Claudia asked curiously, 'What's going on?'

'There's a circus in the park,' the girl told her, 'and some of the clowns have come in to amuse the children. Those who are well enough to join in are having a great time. All the staff are wearing red noses to get into the spirit of the thing.'

As Claudia pushed open the ward doors she saw what the girl meant. A brightly painted organ was churning out music and a tall thin clown was offering Jess Richardson a bunch of paper flowers that he'd just produced from nowhere.

One of his companions was standing on the ward table juggling the fruit from a bowl on one of the lockers, and another had taken over an empty bed and was giving himself medicine from a huge bottle with a rubber spoon.

The children were shrieking their delight and Robin and the rest of the staff, all wearing red plastic noses, were watching the clowns with equal enjoyment.

Her spirits lifted. This was what it was all about. These children with their broken bones, joint deformities, sarcomas and other bodily blights were what mattered. Not the self-pity and frustrations of the adult mind. Leaving this place would be self-inflicted punishment.

The clown on the table had seen her come in and he jumped down and came towards her, his enormous shoes flapping on the tiled floor. He bowed low and offered her a red nose and, entering into the spirit of the thing, Claudia put it on amid cheers from the children.

Then, taking her by surprise, he began to waltz her down the centre of the ward and it was at that moment, with the ward in an uproar, that Lucas came in with Marina and a pallid Peter.

Involved in trying to avoid tripping over the clown's flipper-like shoes, Claudia hadn't seen them, but when a child in one of the beds cried, 'The clowns have come to see us, Dr Morrison!' she turned her head and saw him standing just a few feet away.

'So I see,' he said with a quizzical smile. 'Have they got any red noses to spare?'

Claudia's eyes brightened. This was the Lucas she'd fallen in love with, just as much as the mesmeric charmer, or the tigerish achiever. The children adored him and rightly so. If bedlam was to reign on the unit for a short time it was only fitting that he was part of it.

If it had been Miles Soper who had walked in, there would have been a different response. He believed in being aloof and dignified and it appeared that the dark-haired social worker was the same.

She shook her head when the red nose was offered but her son accepted eagerly and as the merriment went on Claudia's heart continued to lift.

Each time Lucas's dark gaze met hers she sensed that the anger had left him, that here in this ward of sick children they were at peace. There was something else there too, that even Marina's presence couldn't prevent: a message for her alone.

But was she reading it right? Was he really signalling that they had unfinished business? Would he take her to one side when all this was over and tell her...?

What? That he loved her? No chance. He might have been concerned about her safety, critical of what he thought to be her dalliance with a handsome foreigner, but that didn't make him in love with her.

It was just the way he was. Even the memory of the times he'd held her in his arms didn't increase her optimism. They had been merely occasions when the chemistry between them, which they had never denied, had run amok.

The clowns were packing up. Jess Richardson felt that the children had been excited enough for one day. As they left with much waving of hands from small patients and cries of 'Please come back,' the ward gradually became calm again.

Lucas had been the first to go as the Beauchamps were waiting for Peter's tests to be done, which meant that her wild imaginings had been just that. There had been no follow-up to the eye contact. Not even a whispered message that he'd like to talk.

By the time she went to find her car at the end of the

shift those few moments of rapport seemed like a figment of the imagination.

As she went past Dunwoody under the glass-covered entrance hall, Mrs Lewis called, 'I hear that you're leaving, Dr Craven?'

Claudia sighed. She liked the woman and was always ready to pass the time of day with her, but she really didn't want to talk about her decision to leave St Elizabeth's. However...

'Yes, that is so, Mrs Lewis,' she confirmed reluctantly.

'Why is that? You've not been back five minutes.'

'That's true, but I have other plans for the future, I'm afraid.'

'Hmm. Well, you'll be missed.'

'That's nice to know,' she murmured and went on her way.

You're going to have a month of this, she told herself as she pointed herself towards the car-park entrance. Everyone wanting to know why you're leaving...and where you're going, so be prepared.

Someone who had already questioned where she was going and why was walking towards her and Claudia's step faltered. She hadn't seen Lucas since earlier in the day when he'd left the ward with Peter and Marina and now here he was.

'I was hoping I might catch you before you left,' he said without preamble. 'Are you in a rush?'

'Not particularly. Why?'

Claudia was conscious of a breathless sort of feeling, as if with the sight of him reality had receded and fantasy taken over.

It was weeks since he'd sought her out like this, apart from those cool moments in his office at the start of the day, when he'd let her see his annoyance at her impending departure from Lizzie's, but that had been business and this time she had a feeling that it wasn't.

'Have you time to come into my place for a coffee?' he was asking.

Her smile was wry. She had time to fly to the moon with him if he so desired.

'Yes, I think so.'

Play it cool, a voice inside was saying. Just because you and he had a few moments of eye contact this morning and he was happy and carefree for once, don't read too much into it.

The coffee was already percolating when she went in and Claudia wondered if he had been that sure she would come.

'Let me take your coat,' he offered, and went behind to help her remove it.

She could feel his warm breath on the back of her neck and his hands brushing against her shoulders as he eased off the long black leather coat and hung it up.

'You're trembling,' he said teasingly. 'Are you cold? Or is it the fear of finding yourself in the tiger's den?'

It might have been smart to tell him that people had been known to tremble with anticipation, but that would be taking the initiative and she didn't want to do that. He had deliberately waylaid her and first she wanted to know why.

Her curiosity was about to be satisfied.

When he had seated her beside the fire with a cup of steaming coffee Lucas said casually, 'It occurred to me this morning when we were all cavorting about with the clowns that maybe we could have a farewell meal before you depart. What do you think?'

So that was it, she thought glumly. He wanted there to be no loose ends to their relationship. Maybe this was the routine when staff left his unit. A meal out with the chief would create good feelings in the departing member and he would be seen to have done his bit for staff relations.

'Yes, why not?' she agreed airily. 'When do you suggest?'

'Saturday night?'

'All right, but I am at Lizzie's for another three and a half weeks, you know.'

'Yes, I do, but I have a very busy time ahead of me and thought that this coming Saturday was best.'

Claudia got to her feet. 'If it's a struggle to fit me in, forget it. I don't have to have the traditional pat on the head and the ''God go with you'' scenario.'

It was his turn to spring to his feet and as they faced each other it sparked again, the fusion that only seemed to come when they were in dispute.

'Do you have to be so damned awkward?' he gritted as he reached out for her. 'You're the most unpredictable woman I've ever met.'

'Huh! Tell me about it!' she cried as his arms imprisoned her.

'Have no fear. I'm going to. I'm referring to your misleading me about Omar's son, for one thing, and, for another, waiting until the moment my back is turned to decide that you're leaving Lizzie's.'

'You ask for all you get, Lucas.'

'Really? In that case I think it's time I stopped asking and began taking.'

'What do you mean?'

'This,' he murmured with his lips at her throat and his hands moving down her spine. 'I can't stay on a diet for ever, Claudia.'

His touch was inflaming her senses, the heat of his hands burning through her clothes like branding fire, but she wasn't so mesmerised that she hadn't noticed there was no mention of love or commitment.

He'd brought her in here to invite her out for a meal and now he was on about another kind of food, and there was no way she was going to be used for starters when someone else was the main dish.

'I'm going, Lucas,' she said pushing him away. 'It's this kind of thing, amongst others, that has made me decide to leave.'

'You little prude,' he said coldly. 'You know damn well that you want me to make love to you.'

'Maybe I do,' she admitted with equal frostiness, 'but not on these terms.'

CHAPTER NINE

THE tests carried out on Peter Beauchamp were encouraging. The spread of the cancer had been arrested, which meant that radiotherapy and the anti-cancer drugs were having effect. It would be some time before the boy and his mother could be promised a cure but the outlook was improving.

Lucas had previously warned them that the affected bone could easily fracture, but with the lessening of the sarcoma the possibility of that occurring would recede.

It was always heart-warming to be able to tell a patient and their relatives that progress was being made, especially when the illness was so serious. In this case it had been even more pleasurable because he knew the people in question and had strong concerns regarding their welfare.

He had intended imparting the good news to Claudia when he'd coaxed her in for a coffee, but as usual a situation that he'd intended to be in control of had got out of hand.

Once again they had parted with unanswered questions between them, and as Lucas stood looking out on to the dark night after she'd gone he was wishing that he hadn't rushed the suggestion of them having a farewell meal—and hadn't made it sound as if he was fitting her into his spare time as a favour.

He'd suggested the coming Saturday because he had a feeling that everything was getting out of control, that bridges needed to be mended and the sooner the better.

Why was it that with her he never seemed to get it right?

He could handle staff with his eyes shut. They rallied round him like troops to battle, but Claudia Craven was more likely to be against him, rather than for him.

Belinda's words kept coming into his mind. She'd said that Claudia was too vulnerable to be contemplating going to some war-torn land...that she needed Lizzie's at this time in her life.

He agreed wholeheartedly. She certainly needed something or someone, and for the first time in his life he admitted that so did he.

Walking across to the hospital the next morning in early May sunshine, Lucas was determined to act on the resolve he'd made late the previous night.

As soon as the restaurant he'd chosen was likely to be open he was going to book the meal for Saturday night as if there had been no confrontation between them regarding it.

If Claudia refused to go he would either have to coax or command, one or the other, and take his chances.

He wasn't to know that she was just as anxious to see him the moment she arrived, but it wasn't about that.

The results of Peter's tests could be had from other people but she wanted to hear it from Lucas. Whatever his relationship was with Marina, she knew that he was deeply concerned over the boy and so was she.

She found him studying X-ray plates in the ward office with Jess Richardson. 'Good morning, Dr Craven,' he said smoothly. 'Still being tempted by the enticements of spring?'

What was that supposed to mean? she wondered. That if she wasn't to be tempted by his enticements, maybe the weather would turn her on?

'Absolutely!' she gushed. 'Nothing can equal the English spring.'

The ward sister was eyeing them both as if she thought they'd lost their minds and Claudia hid a smile. Jess really would think they were crazy if she knew that only a few short hours ago they'd been in each other's arms.

Lucas was pointing to the X-ray plate. 'What does that suggest?'

'A sternomastoid lump in the neck?' she said cautiously after making a careful examination.

'Correct. It's torticollis, or wryneck as it's sometimes known. This infant was found to have the problem at an early age and has been having the neck exercised in an attempt to straighten the shortened muscle, along with advice to the parents to put the child on alternate sides when sleeping, but it hasn't worked. So have you any suggestions?'

Claudia's glance went back to the X-ray plate. 'Er...yes. I think so. Surgery to divide the tendon that is causing the trouble?'

He smiled. 'Correct again. I really am going to miss having you around the wards.'

She had no answering smile to that. It was an accurate description of where, and how much, she mattered.

'About Peter,' she said as they prepared to leave the office. 'What were the test results?'

'Good,' he said briefly. 'A ray of light in darkness.'

'Oh! I'm so thankful for them both.'

Lucas nodded. 'We all are, but I don't need to tell you that he's a long way to go, do I?'

'No, of course not.'

They were approaching the first bed and, before he stopped to pick up the small patient's notes, he said casually, 'I've booked the meal for Saturday.'

It wasn't strictly true as the restaurant wouldn't be open yet, but he'd thought, Why not put out a feeler...test the water?

Typically the response wasn't what he'd expected. 'Fine,' she said carelessly. 'What time did we say?'

'We didn't. We got sidetracked, if you remember?'

'Ah! Yes, we did,' she agreed without taking him up on the comment. 'So what time have you booked the meal for?'

Something glinted in his eyes. It could have been amusement, or annoyance more likely, because today she was being irritatingly malleable. Whatever it was, she wasn't destined to find out.

'I've made a reservation for seven-thirty. I'll call for you around sevenish.'

His bleeper went before she could reply and his face was serious as he took the message, 'That was Accident and Emergency. They want me down there. I'll leave you to do the rounds,' and, with his habitual vigour restored, he departed.

If Lucas had been surprised at her capitulation over his invitation she supposed it was understandable. He hadn't been the only one who had spent some time thinking after their cool goodbyes.

In almost a month's time she would be gone, Claudia had reminded herself, so why not make the best of what was left? If Lucas was in a hurry to bid her farewell, so be it, but at least they would have a few hours together on Saturday night, whatever the reason for him suggesting it.

Therefore when he had mentioned it again today she had taken the wind out of his sails by acting as if she were taking it for granted that the invitation still stood.

*   *   *

The day that had started with the vestige of a truce between them took its course. Lucas hadn't returned since being called to the emergency down below and it was Robin's day off, so Claudia was the only doctor on the wards.

Raised voices outside in the corridor diverted her attention from Hannah Horrocks, who was finding the plaster cast that she'd had fitted after her operation restrictive and itchy. Leaving the child for a moment, she went outside to investigate.

A man was running towards her with a charge nurse from one of the other wards some distance behind him crying, 'Stop him! He's broken into the drugs cupboard!'

Anger erupted inside her. How dared this thief take the medicines needed for sick children? Incredibly there was no one else in sight and the nurse was too far behind to catch him. It was up to her.

Surprise flickered in his eyes as she blocked his path, and as he hesitated for a second the black bin-bag in his hand swung to and fro. Then he was swiping at her with his free arm, but Claudia was not to be so easily dismissed. She hung onto him like a limpet, but just as the breathless charge nurse caught up with him he broke free and, knocking Claudia to the ground, he ran off, right into the arms of Lucas and a hospital security guard.

They must have been pre-warned for while the guard pinned the miscreant up against the wall, Lucas ran to where Claudia was lying on the hard tiled floor with her leg bent awkwardly beneath her.

The look of horrified concern on his face was balm to her soul but his angry remonstrations were not.

'What the hell did you think you were doing?' he yelled, dropping to his knees beside her. 'Tackling that thug! You could have been killed!'

She gave a little moan and he ordered, 'Don't try to move your leg, Claudia. It looks as if it's broken.'

When she'd needed some help the corridor had been deserted, but now it was full of people, nursing staff, visitors and security men appearing from all directions, with Lucas, white-faced and angry, supervising her transfer to the X-ray unit.

As the pain in her leg increased and shock from the fall began to take effect Claudia started to shake and he eyed her anxiously.

'A cup of hot sweet tea, please, Nurse,' he requested of Sheila Newcome who was accompanying them to X-ray in a state of complete disbelief.

She nodded and was gone, leaving Claudia to wonder how her life could have changed so drastically in just a few seconds. One moment she'd been a doctor on ward rounds, the next face to face with a criminal, and now, her role reversed, she was going to end up as a patient.

In spite of her distress the thought brought a smile to her face. At least she'd hurt herself in a manner that would keep Lucas in her orbit, even though his expression was hardly that of the commiserating colleague.

Lucas saw the smile as he strode along beside the hospital trolley that a young porter was pushing and he raised his eyes heavenwards.

'You really are something else!' he gritted. 'You rush into danger without a second thought, almost get yourself killed, sustain what could be a serious fracture in the process...and yet find something to smile about, while *I* nearly had a heart attack.'

In her present state smiles and tears were not far apart and her eyes filled at his angry criticism. 'Why do you keep shouting at me?' she choked. 'I was only doing what I thought was right. You would have done the same.'

'I'm angry because you put yourself at such risk. You are a constant thorn in my side, but life without you would be unbearable. Does that answer the question?'

Claudia closed her eyes. Was that supposed to be a crumb of consolation? He was saying that he'd be desolate if anything had happened to her, but now that she was safe he was entitled to express his irritation at what she'd done.

With the devil at her elbow she said, 'If you're acting like this because I'm increasing your workload, perhaps Miles Soper will sort out my injury?'

Claudia watched a red tide of anger ride from his neck until it was suffusing his cheeks and wondered why she was letting him get to her like this when she was feeling so dreadful.

'You will have the best,' he snapped, 'and that's me! Do you honestly think I would trust you to anyone else?'

'No. I suppose not,' she replied wearily.

'You suppose not! You should know that to be the case beyond any doubt, never mind supposing—and, Claudia, if the fracture is as serious as I think it might be, you're not going to have much to smile about, my darling.'

She knew that she must have had a knock on the head as well as a suspected fracture. Lucas had called her his darling. Had she imagined it, or had it been a slip of the tongue?

Claudia had sustained a Pott's fracture, combining breakage of the tibia and fibula, with dislocation of the ankle.

'Needless to say, I'm going to have to operate,' Lucas told her sombrely when he'd viewed the X-ray plates, 'not only to manipulate the bones back into position, but there are fragments of bone there that will need screwing into place.'

At that moment the agony was being held in check with

painkillers, but it would soon be back and once she had assimilated the bleak tidings Claudia wanted to know, 'How soon can you do it?'

'They're getting the theatre ready now,' he replied.

At that moment they were one doctor talking to another, not friends, or lovers, just a couple of medics discussing a case, but in this instance one of them was the patient.

Her last memory of Lucas before she slid into oblivion was of cool eyes above blue theatre pyjamas and steady hands that were waiting to make her mobile again.

He'd bent over her in those last few seconds and touched her cheek and she'd gone into limbo with a smile on her lips.

He was beside her when she surfaced again in the recovery unit and she mumbled blearily, 'Haven't you got work to do?'

'Yes, I have, but first I had to make sure that my private patient was back with us and conscious enough to understand what is going to happen next.

'If this wasn't a children's hospital I'd keep you in, but, seeing that it is, I can't do that. However, there are some alternatives.'

Claudia's head was clearing, her mind tuning in. She eyed him thoughtfully. What was coming next?

'As you live alone we could transfer you to another hospital for a few days. Or you could go to your parents' place for a while. Another alternative is that you could return to your flat and hope that the plaster cast you're going to be wearing won't be too cumbersome to cope with.'

'I'll still be in plaster when I leave Lizzie's, won't I?'

She saw him wince, but his voice was calm enough as

he replied, 'Yes, you will. It will be the usual eight to ten weeks for a Pott's fracture.'

'I don't see why anything need change,' she told him. 'I'll go back to my apartment. I can manage to hobble about on crutches.'

'I don't know if your parents would be happy about that. I'm certainly not.' He hesitated. 'How about being my guest for a few days? I could keep an eye on you.'

Don't tempt me! she wanted to cry. But that really would be too embarrassing, having Lucas looking after her, and in any case she would manage.

'Thanks just the same,' she said, 'but I'd like to try on my own. The biggest problem will be not being able to drive here.'

'What do you mean—drive here?' he asked with raised brows.

'To Lizzie's.'

'You're surely not contemplating working with a combined fracture of the leg and a dislocated ankle?'

'I'm going to give it a try.'

'You have to have my permission first.'

'And?'

'No way.' He got to his feet. 'And, in the meantime, you stay where you are and the moment I'm free I'll take you home…much against my better judgement.'

The unaccustomed plaster cast felt heavy and cumbersome as Lucas put her key in the lock of the apartment and stood back to let her propel herself inside.

She was feeling weak and disorientated and was already wishing herself anywhere but in the place where she was going to have to cope alone.

With his incredible insight into her mind he was already tuned into her dismal thoughts, but instead of sympathising he said briskly, 'I'll make us a meal. You'll feel better when you've eaten and then it's off to bed with you—and whether you like it or not, Claudia, I'm staying the night. I can sleep on the couch and when morning comes we'll see how you are. OK?'

'I suppose so,' she agreed dejectedly.

How many times had she imagined the two of them here? Eating together, showering together, sleeping to-gether—and now it had happened. Lucas was actually here in her apartment and she...she had a huge plaster cast on her leg, bruises by the score, and she felt like death.

'What happened to the thief?' she asked as she ate the quick snack he prepared.

'The police came and took him away. Apparently there's been a series of drug thefts during recent weeks, so they're hoping that this will put an end to it. Unless he has accomplices.'

She was praying that he wouldn't start harping about the risk she'd taken. It was over now. She'd paid for it with broken bones, but at least a bagful of drugs would be back where they belonged.

He didn't. Instead Lucas said, 'Do you mind if I give Marina a quick ring? I'd promised to take her and the boy to a show tonight and they'll be wondering what's hap-pened to me if I don't turn up.'

'Yes, do, by all means,' she said stiffly, thinking that he must be bored out of his mind at the thought of playing nursemaid to herself when he could have been living it up in the West end with the Beauchamps.

The phone was in the hall so she didn't hear what he said to Marina, but when he came back into the room he was smiling.

'I've just had some good news,' he said buoyantly.

'Really?' she commented flatly. 'I'll leave you to your

pleasure, then. There are blankets and pillows in the hall cupboard. I'll see you in the morning,' and before he had time to say anything that would depress her further she went hobbling off to the comfort of her virgin bed, feeling unlovely and unloved.

When Claudia awoke the next morning the plaster cast on her leg was an instant reminder of the happenings of the previous day and with the memory came a riot of emotions.

In spite of her exhaustion she had been a long time in sleeping after leaving Lucas to dwell on whatever it was that had pleased him so.

She'd listened to him moving about the apartment as he'd made up a bed on the sofa and had ached for the comfort of his arms around her, but common sense had told her that, concerned though he might be about her, it didn't make him in love with her.

If she were to hobble out of the bedroom seeking solace, dressed only in a silk nightgown, the passion that arose so swiftly between them might be kindled again and she wasn't seeking that.

It was tenderness and reassurance she needed, but maybe she'd been too intent on showing him that she was a modern woman, self-sufficient, and capable of steering her own ship, which she was...most of the time.

She'd slept at last but there had been no depth to her slumbers, until at last in a pearly dawn she had found oblivion.

And now, wide awake, with the memory that Lucas had been sleeping just a few feet away making her blood run warm, she braced herself to face the day ahead. She had a serious leg fracture and was very aware that last night she'd left the man she wanted in her life in a state of elation—and it seemed his elation was not connected with herself.

Maybe Marina had said 'yes'. Perhaps that was why he'd been keeping the state of his relationship with her under wraps. He'd been waiting for her to make up her mind.

As Claudia struggled into a towelling robe and flicked a brush through her hair there were no sounds coming from the sitting room. For a moment she wondered if he'd gone, departing at daybreak after having given up his night to her.

As she pushed the door open slowly it was evident that he'd done no such thing. Lucas was fast asleep, lying face down on top of the covers in the breath-taking nakedness of the healthy, attractive male, with arms outflung and one leg hanging over the edge of the sofa.

He looked oddly young and vulnerable and her heartbeat quickened. She would have loved to have known him when he was a boy, the determined young toughie who was going places no matter what, just as she wanted to know more of the man he had become, but they seemed to be at odds all the time. Conflict of personalities, she'd called it, but it didn't have to be that way if they could only talk—and if Marina Beauchamp would emigrate!

Claudia longed to touch him, to trace her fingers along his spine, to stroke the firm buttocks and press her cheek against the broad shoulders, but he would most surely waken at the contact and then what would she say if he repulsed her?

As she was pouring a glass of juice he appeared behind her, padding silently across the kitchen floor on bare feet, but the rest of him was no longer bare.

Her face warmed as she realised that he must have been aware of her presence in the other room, as it was only seconds since she'd left and here he was dressed in his clothes from yesterday.

'And how are you this morning?' he asked with his eyes on her plastered leg.

'A bit sore and bruised and the plaster takes some getting used to, but apart from that I'm not too bad.'

'Did you sleep?'

'Er…yes…after a fashion. Did you?'

'Like a baby.'

That would be because he was happy, she thought dismally. It was only those feeling miserable that found sleep hard to come by.

'So. Keep off the leg as much as you can for the next few days,' Lucas was suggesting, 'and I'll see you at the fracture clinic on Friday.'

'You mean to say I'm not to report for work?'

He sighed. 'Of course not! I've already told you. Are you crazy?'

'So I won't be back on the wards before I leave Lizzie's?'

His face tightened. 'You understand me exactly. But that doesn't mean to say we have to cancel our dinner appointment for Saturday, does it?'

Was there a note of entreaty in his voice? She must be imagining it. Lucas Morrison wasn't in the habit of pleading.

'No, I suppose not,' she replied. 'Will you pick me up, as the Boxter is going to be standing idle for the next few weeks?'

'Yes, of course. But I'll be seeing you before then at the clinic.'

Lucas was fixing his tie with one eye on the clock and gulping down the juice that she'd poured for him at the same time as her own. Soon he would be gone, back to the busy hospital that she was barred from after yesterday.

He paused at the front door with briefcase in hand and looked down at her. 'Take care of yourself, Claudia,' he said soberly. 'That incident yesterday was serious enough, but it could have been so much worse if the fellow had been armed.'

She nodded meekly. 'Yes, I know.'

No point in telling him that she would do the same thing again.

'And, Lucas, thanks for operating on my leg and for staying with me last night. I know that you had other plans and it must have been a bind for you having to cancel them.'

He dropped the briefcase and took her face between his hands. 'None of that matters, Claudia, as long as you are safe.' Bending, he kissed her briefly on the lips.

It wasn't like the other times he'd kissed her. It was a consoling sort of gesture, platonic almost, but the moment their mouths made contact it changed and they were clinging together as if he were departing to the other side of the world rather than a few miles up the road.

'What would you have done if I'd rolled over and grabbed you in the livingroom?' he asked when at last she sagged against him limply.

'Asked you what your intentions were…or hit you with one of my crutches,' she said weakly.

'You wouldn't have needed to look far for proof of my intentions,' he teased, 'but I don't take advantage of women on crutches.'

He was bending to pick up his discarded case and straightening his tie. 'Lizzie's calls. I must go—and remember, Claudia, no confrontations with strange men.'

As the magic of the moment dribbled away she turned

to go back inside, telling him as she did so, 'I work with one. Didn't you know?'

Robin phoned during the morning to offer his commiserations and to enquire how she was, and shortly afterwards there was a call from Belinda.

'How's the leg?' her friend asked. 'I was horrified when I heard what had happened.'

'It's not too uncomfortable,' Claudia told her, 'but then I was lucky enough to have the best when it came to operating. About that, there's something I need to know, Belinda.'

There was a pause and then Lucas's secretary said slowly, 'What is it?'

'Is Lucas going to get into trouble for using Lizzie's facilities to treat me?'

'I had a feeling you were going to ask me that,' she replied. 'Do you want the truth?'

'Yes, of course I do.'

'He's already been called to account for his actions by the hospital hierarchy, who are saying that as St Elizabeth's is a paediatric hospital he should have had you transferred elsewhere for treatment.

'Needless to say he is less than impressed, especially as you were injured on the hospital's behalf. He's told them that as far as his services are concerned you were a private patient and if the hospital wants to charge him for use of the theatre and the services of the staff who assisted, he will settle the account.'

Claudia groaned. Whenever they were involved in anything together it was a catastrophe. Lucas had done what he would have done for any friend or acquaintance, and now he was being rebuked for it. He must see her as the biggest millstone of all time.

'There's no malice on the part of the hospital authority,' Belinda was assuring her. 'You're the heroine of the day and will be receiving a special acknowledgement, but everything has to be done by the book.'

'Is he there?' she asked. 'I need to discuss it with him.'

'No. He's in theatre at the moment, but I can ask him to give you a ring when he's free.'

'Yes, if you would,' Claudia agreed.

When Belinda had gone off the line Claudia sat staring into space. Obviously she would meet any costs herself. There was no way that Lucas was going to have another burden thrust upon him—certainly not from her. If it was too much to pay herself, her father would pay it, and on that thought she decided that it was time to tell her parents what had happened yesterday.

They were horrified and urged her to come home immediately. 'We'll come and pick you up, darling,' her mother said. 'If you're not able to go to work you might as well spend some time here.'

'No, Mum,' she said. 'I want to stay here. I've given in my notice but don't finish officially for three weeks and during that time I want to be in the area.'

She didn't want to tell her mother that she was wishing she hadn't been so hasty, or that she wanted to be around to keep a dinner appointment at the weekend.

'Why have you decided to leave St Elizabeth's?' her mother wanted to know. 'Is it something to do with Lucas Morrison?'

'It has everything to do with him.'

'I see. Well, Claudia, I would still like you to come home, but if that is what you want, we understand.' Her voice rose. 'The man must be blind if he can't see that you were made for each other!'

'Or else he only sees what he wants to see,' Claudia finished glumly.

Lucas didn't phone and, as there was no way that she wanted to make a nuisance of herself when he was busy, Claudia fretted through the long day.

By the time six o'clock came she was almost wishing she'd gone home as her parents had suggested, but common sense said that she would feel even more frustrated hidden away in the Cotswolds.

She was seated at the kitchen table picking at an omelette when the doorbell rang and with the aid of the crutches she moved slowly to answer it.

Lucas was holding the familiar brown carrier bag of the take-away in his hand and eyeing her keenly as he said with his sardonic smile, 'Can I come in? I've brought my own food and some for you as well, if you haven't eaten.'

Her spirits were rising by the minute. The depressing day was as if it had never existed. He was lighting up her life once again.

As she stepped back clumsily to let him in Claudia was wishing that she'd changed out of the sloppy old jumper and long skirt that she'd been slouching around in all day, but it was too late now and what did it matter? He was here. Lucas had taken the time to come to her at the end of his busy day.

'So are you going to join me?' he was asking as he put the bag on the table and took off his jacket.

She nodded. Not surprisingly her appetite was back and, scraping the remains of the omelette into the waste bin, she produced knives and forks and they began to eat.

'Apart from a ham sandwich at lunch-time this is the first bite I've had all day,' he informed her. 'We're really missing you on the wards, Claudia.'

She saw the opening and jumped into it. 'I don't see why I couldn't report for duty. As long as no one objects to my lack of mobility.'

Lucas shook his head. 'I think not. When I said we were missing you it wasn't a hint that I want you back at Lizzie's.'

His face was bleak. 'In any case you will be missing permanently soon and we'll have to manage then.'

She swallowed hard. Was this the moment to tell him that she'd made a mistake? That she didn't want to go?

If it was, he was forestalling her. 'The clinical tutor wasn't very pleased when you handed in your notice after such a short time, but he's happy enough now as he's found a replacement.'

So there was no turning back. Not without making herself look a prize idiot.

'There is something I need to talk about, Lucas,' she said into the silence that followed.

'Yes?' he questioned, dark eyes immediately alert, making her wonder what he was expecting it to be.

'I spoke to Belinda this morning and she told me that you are being harassed by the hospital authority for treating me inside Lizzie's.'

His face had tightened and he'd tutted angrily while she'd been speaking. 'She had no right! The dispute is between myself and them. You don't come into it.'

'But I do! Of course I do! If it wasn't for me you wouldn't be having this problem.'

'If it wasn't for a greedy thief, you mean! None of it has to concern you, Claudia. So let's leave it at that.'

'No!' she persisted. 'I can't do that. If you won't let me pay you for your services, at least let me pay for the rest of it when they send you the account.'

He was on his feet, anger in every line of him. 'That

does it! I've heard it all! A member of my staff is hurt during working hours and she thinks I might want paying for helping her. Then, adding insult to injury, ''Miss Moneybags'' decides to patronize me by offering to get me out of the mess.

'Is it too much for you to take in that I might have done it because I was so humbly grateful to find you more or less in one piece...that I would have given the shirt off my back to have you safe...and that I don't care a damn about being in the dog house?

'Money doesn't come into it, Claudia. Except for the times when you start flashing it around in the manner of those to whom it comes easily.'

'Who's being insulting now?' she cried. 'It's a wonder you don't trip over the enormous chip on your shoulder. I was only trying to help!'

Her words were wasted. With one last angry look he had gone.

CHAPTER TEN

ON FRIDAY afternoon the appointment's clerk at the fracture clinic said, 'Go right in, Dr Craven. It's the great man himself and your friend Robin Crawshaw doing the honours today.'

Claudia shook her head. 'I'd rather wait my turn. Thanks just the same.'

She'd phoned Belinda the previous day to make sure it wouldn't create any further problems, protocol-wise, if she attended the clinic at St Elizabeth's, and her friend had told her sympathetically, 'It will create problems if you don't attend, Claudia. A certain person that we both hold in high regard will not be happy if you don't put in an appearance.'

'Even though he's already in trouble with the authorities on my account?'

'Yes. He's been like a bear with a sore head this week, which does make one inclined to think that he is missing you.'

'I doubt it,' she'd rejoined drily. 'Lucas nearly went berserk when I offered to pay any expenses from my treatment.'

Belinda had laughed. 'Well, he would, wouldn't he? The man has pride...and you *are* his star pupil.'

'Past tense,' she'd said dolefully. 'I won't be back at Lizzie's again. I'll be leaving before the plaster comes off.'

'What is the actual date of your departure?'

'The last Friday in May.'

'I thought it might be.'

'Why?'

'Lucas has got a black circle around it on his calendar.'

'With "Hurrah!" above it?'

'No, of course not. You've got him all wrong, Claudia.'

'I wish I could believe that,' she'd said wistfully.

And now she was about to find out if the cold zone was still in operation.

'I told them to send you straight in,' he said when she appeared.

'Yes, I know, but I preferred to wait my turn.'

'I see. So how's the leg been?'

'All right.'

'No pain or discomfort?'

'Very little.'

'Fine. So if you'll pop along to X-ray we'll have it checked out.'

As she rose to do his bidding it seemed unreal. This was the doctor-patient routine at its most extreme. Anyone watching would think they were strangers.

Not so with Robin when he saw her. 'Claudia!' he cried, beaming his pleasure. 'How goes it?'

'All right,' she told him with an answering smile. It was hardly the place to tell him that she was miserable and lonely.

'It's deadly on the wards without you,' he confided. 'Lucas is so morose it just isn't true. Even the voluptuous widow can't get a smile out of him.'

'He probably keeps them for when they're alone,' she said flatly. 'But what about you? How's your romance going?'

His colour was rising. 'Carolyn wants us to get engaged.'

'And are you going to?'

'Hmm.'

'Good for you. I think…'

'Are you intending going to X-ray?' Lucas asked tightly as he approached from the rear.

'Er…yes…of course,' she mumbled. 'Bye for now, Robin.'

By the time she'd been dealt with and hobbled back to see Lucas the clinic was empty and she found him sitting at his desk staring into space.

'Ah! At last,' he remarked drily as she put the plates on his desk. 'I thought I was going to have to organise a search party.'

'There were a lot of people waiting,' she said stiffly. 'I'm sorry if I've delayed you.'

'You haven't. I popped into Neurology while I was waiting for you to come back, to speak to one of the doctors there, as I have a child about to be admitted who has other problems besides orthopaedic, and since I've come back I've been pondering on the complexities of the human race.'

'In what way?'

'There is a youngster in one of their side wards seriously ill with bacterial meningitis. He has been transferred from another hospital some miles away for more specialised care.

'The doctor who is treating him was telling me that his parents are totally devastated, in a state of complete despair, which is not surprising. Yet when the other hospital offered to arrange transport for them, so that they could be with him here, they declined, saying that they were going home. In other words they've given up on the little chap.'

'Maybe they feel shut out,' she suggested. 'That where before their child depended on them, now they are useless.

Somebody else has taken over and they can't cope with being on the sidelines.'

'Could be, I suppose,' he said doubtfully, 'but it's not the attitude of most people. If someone we care for is seriously ill and might die, we feel the need to be with them every waking moment.

'But let's get back to you, Claudia. I've got a couple of hours free so I'll drive you home.'

'What?' she cried. 'You hadn't a civil word for me when I arrived and now you're offering to drive me home? Make up your mind, Lucas—am I out in the cold, or not?'

He was examining the X-ray plates and as he turned back to her he was smiling. 'No problems there. What was it you were saying?'

'Nothing! Nothing at all!'

'Right, so let's go, shall we?'

Claudia knew she was being spineless letting him take her home. She should have told him where to go in no uncertain terms after his brusque manner at the clinic, but this was how it was with them. They couldn't agree when they were together and yet they were miserable apart.

'I can't stay,' he said when he stopped the car in front of her apartment.

She was tempted to tell him that she hadn't asked him to, but she sensed that there was something else.

'I've been invited to an engagement party tonight and am going home to get changed.'

'Marriage must be in the air,' she said with an attempt at flippancy. 'First Robin has been telling me that he's contemplating getting engaged and now you've been asked to help someone celebrate the event. Spring certainly is a very romantic time.'

His sardonic smile was there. 'Any time is a romantic time if love is there…as we both know. The only trouble is that sometimes it is buried so deep that one, or both, of the lovers don't recognise its presence.'

Claudia became still. What was he telling her? Dared she let hope be born again? She shook her head as she began to ease herself slowly out of the car. There was no way of knowing if Lucas was generalising and, if recent events were anything to go by, he probably was.

If he read her thoughts he gave no sign of it. Instead he said casually, 'Seven o'clock tomorrow, then?' and as she gaped at him, 'You hadn't forgotten?'

'No, I hadn't forgotten, but after the other night's crossing of swords I wasn't expecting…'

'That was then, this is now, and tomorrow is another day, Claudia,' he said calmly, and with a careless wave of the hand he went.

Supported by the crutches, she watched the car go out of sight, already pondering on what to wear for an occasion that she hadn't been expecting to happen.

Whatever she wore on the top half, the obvious choice for the bottom was something long and loose to cover her bulky leg.

Black suited her. It enhanced her golden fairness, and after studying the contents of her wardrobe she decided on a flowing skirt with a dipped waistband and the black sequinned top with long, tight sleeves and low cut at the front.

It was an outfit she'd worn before and she knew it made her look older and extremely sophisticated, which was the effect she desired.

Tomorrow night she wanted Lucas to see her in a different light. She was no longer a junior doctor obeying his every command, but a woman of the world who had known joy and sorrow and then joy again, only to find the new joy a confusing emotion.

It wasn't as simple as the gentle affection that she and Jack had felt for each other. Loving Lucas Morrison was like being swept along by a whirlwind one moment and the next walking on quicksands and she didn't want it to be like that.

She had the measure of the man, knew his strength, his weaknesses, and wanted to be part of his life, but he had to be ready to let her into it, and, in spite of him continually seeking her out, Claudia sensed his reservations about their relationship.

He was wary of committing himself to her for one very good reason—Marina Beauchamp—and with the thought of her the memory of his euphoria the other night came back. What was the 'good news' that had pleased him so greatly? she wondered.

Belinda came round on Saturday morning to see if she could shop for her and after Claudia had accepted gratefully the two women sat chatting over coffee.

'How did it go at the fracture clinic?' her friend wanted to know.

'Fine. Lucas brought me home afterwards.'

'Really? So am I to take it that there is a truce?'

'We're always having truces, but I'm afraid they don't last. He's taking me for a farewell meal tonight.'

'It's a bit previous, isn't it, if you aren't officially leaving Lizzie's until the end of the month?'

Claudia nodded. 'That's what I said, but the reason he gave was that it's the only time he's free, which makes me think he must have a very active social life, or he wants to get it over and done with. Apparently it's standard procedure with him to take out members of staff when they're leaving.'

'It's news to me!' Belinda exclaimed. 'I've been his

secretary for some time and I don't recall it happening before, though, come to think of it, I can't remember anyone leaving since he came.'

'Except me?'

'Yes. You're the first. The rest of the staff are devoted to him. Miles Soper they tolerate, but Lucas is in a class of his own.'

When Belinda had gone to the supermarket to pick up her groceries Claudia went over the conversation. It didn't help one bit to hear Belinda eulogising over Lucas. She didn't have to be told about his excellence. She'd seen it with her own eyes.

It was a pity that it didn't spill over into his relationship with herself. If the day ever dawned when she understood what was in his mind there would be a flag flying from her roof-top.

She was ready for their dinner date in plenty of time. Since injuring her leg nothing was easy when it came to movement, and so extra minutes had to be allowed for washing and dressing, and as she moved slowly around the apartment Claudia was wishing she could put the clock back in more ways than one.

If she hadn't fractured her leg she would still be working at Lizzie's and Lucas wouldn't be in trouble with the hospital authorities, and if that weren't so they wouldn't have quarrelled the other night.

It was an ongoing catastrophe and she couldn't see any end to it, but at least there was one light in the darkness. Tonight she was going to dazzle him. Cast a spell on him in the intimate atmosphere of the restaurant that would make everything fall into place.

'Marina Beauchamp, eat your heart out!' she told the absent widow.

Apart from the fact that on one foot she was wearing a low-heeled silver sandal and on the other nothing but the plaster cast, the final effect was stunning, and as the minutes ticked by the feeling of anticipation increased.

Seven o'clock had been and gone but she wasn't too bothered. A few minutes either way didn't matter. By seven-fifteen she was frowning and by half-past, when they should have been at their table in the restaurant, she was completely disconcerted.

If the car had broken down or an emergency had arisen at Lizzie's, Lucas would surely have phoned. How could he leave her like this in a state of limbo, dressed to kill, and nowhere to go?

At eight o'clock she rang his flat but there was no answer. Then she phoned the hospital but all was calm there, no crisis that might need an orthopaedic surgeon.

An hour later she got in touch with the police to check if there had been any accidents in the area through which he would have driven to get to her, and was reassured to find that there hadn't.

Anxiety and anger were churning side by side inside her. If Lucas had been delayed why hadn't he let her know? He was the one who'd been pushing for this meeting, determined that it should go ahead in spite of their differences in recent days. So why wasn't he here?

If he'd gone to see Marina that would be it. She certainly had her own slot in his life and maybe it was time that she, Claudia, discovered exactly how much the woman meant to him. She'd fretted long enough.

On impulse she dialled Marina's number, not sure what she was going to say when she answered, but driven to do it nevertheless.

A man's voice came over the line and Claudia went

rigid, until she realised that his accent was similar to her own. There were no northern overtones to it.

'Yes? Who's there?' he was asking.

'Claudia Craven. Can I speak to Marina, please?'

'She isn't here at the moment. I'm her fiancé. Can I take a message?'

'Er…no, thanks. I'll ring back,' she croaked.

'Just as you like,' he replied and the line went dead.

'I've been invited to an engagement party,' Lucas had said and she'd never thought to ask where. Could it have been Marina's?

A huge weight had been lifted off her shoulders. Lucas *wasn't* having a relationship with the other woman unless the pleasant-voiced man who'd just answered the phone was being sadly misled.

She wanted to jump for joy, but that was easier said than done with a fractured leg, and wasn't she forgetting something? If Lucas wasn't with Marina he had to be somewhere else and it certainly wasn't here.

As the minutes ticked by with no sign of him the in-activity was becoming unbearable. If Lucas Morrison promised to do something he did it. He was a man of his word, even if she didn't always agree with his actions. He'd said he would come for her and he hadn't, so something was wrong.

Maybe she ought to seek him out instead of sitting around in a state of acute frustration and anxiety and, following the thought with the deed, she phoned for a taxi.

If Lucas wasn't at his flat when she got there she would have had a wasted journey, but for now it was enough that she was doing something.

When the taxi turned into the complex of hospital flat-lets the first thing Claudia saw was an ambulance outside with lights flashing and doors open wide.

It was hardly an unusual sight in the vicinity of a large hospital and she might have thought nothing of it, except for the fact that it was outside Lucas's place.

Asking the taxi driver to wait, Claudia made her laborious descent from his vehicle, wishing her fractured leg with its cumbersome plaster a million miles away.

The desire to act, to move fast, was so strong within her she could have wept at her inability to do so.

'Keep calm,' she was telling herself as she moved slowly towards the entrance. 'There are other people living here.' But as two paramedics came hurrying out of the building she knew that the dark head, visible above the covers on the trolley they were pushing could only belong to one person.

'Stop, please!' she begged as they made to pass her. 'What's wrong? I'm a doctor...and a friend of his.'

'Can't say, I'm afraid,' one of them informed her cautiously. 'Dr Morrison managed to phone us, complaining of severe head pains. When we got here he was in a collapsed condition.'

Lucas was deathly pale in the light of the street lamps and as Claudia looked down on him her blood ran cold. He was covered in a purple rash.

Her voice must have penetrated his semi-conscious state and he muttered, 'Go away, Claudia. Don't want you to get it.'

'Can't delay, Miss. We've got to get the patient to the nearest hospital,' one of the paramedics said, and without giving her time to reply they wheeled the stretcher into the ambulance and prepared to shut the doors.

'I want to come with you,' she cried.

The same man eyed her crutches. 'You look as if you've got enough problems of your own. Better to follow on in the taxi.'

She nodded. It made sense. She would only delay them in her present state and as the tail-lights of the ambulance disappeared into the night the taxi followed with Claudia crouched in the back seat, paralysed with fear.

One word was thudding inside her head but she dared not say it. She'd seen the rash once before, when she'd first started working on the wards, and, along with the headache and the lapsing in and out of consciousness, all the signs were there.

'Please, God,' she prayed. 'Don't let it be that. Don't let Lucas die!'

In the days that followed her prayers were answered in part. It was meningitis that Lucas had, but he didn't die, even though there were moments during those first few hours when those treating him in an isolation ward in a strange hospital thought that the angel of death was hovering.

For Claudia, waiting anxiously for the moment when she would be told whether he was going to live, the nightmare that had started with the sighting of the ambulance outside his flat went on.

She knew now why he hadn't got in touch with her that night. He had known that if he'd told her he was ill she would have gone rushing round, risking infection.

The onset of the disease must have been swift and sudden but thankfully he had managed to summon help before sinking into unconsciousness.

It was just like him, she thought tenderly as the hours went slowly past. Before this, he'd probably never ailed a thing in his life, but it hadn't stopped him from being concerned about the ills of others. Even as he was being attacked by a disease that was a known killer he'd put her safety first.

She'd had no address for Oliver, but the hospital had managed to contact him at the halls of residence, and when he'd arrived, with eyes huge and anxious in a bleached face, she had known that Lucas would want her to be there for his brother. They had sat together through the first long night, united in their concern.

'I can't believe it,' he'd said. 'Lucas is never ill. Sophie and I have been poorly at times, but never him.'

'Lucas is only human,' she'd said quietly. 'Even the strongest of us are not completely invincible.'

'He's going to die, isn't he?' he'd sobbed.

Her heart had clenched. 'Not if these people in Intensive Care can help it. They're doing all they can.'

She'd persuaded Oliver to go home when it was daylight and with reluctance he'd gone, leaving her to continue the vigil alone.

They hadn't let her see him so far and for that reason she didn't want to move. If there was the slightest chance of her being allowed in, she wanted to be there.

At last it came. 'You can see him for five minutes…wearing a mask and gown,' the consultant neurologist said. 'Dr Morrison is conscious at the moment, but don't tire him by talking. Just let him see that you're here. Your name was the first word on his lips when he surfaced.'

The eyes looking up at her when she went to stand by the bed were dull and lifeless, but he was running true to form. 'Told you to go away,' he said in a slurred whisper. 'Might catch it.'

'I don't care, my darling,' she told him gently. 'Please get better. I love you so.'

'You do?'

'Yes, more than life itself.'

He nodded, wincing at the effort. 'See what I can do, then.'

The doctor was hovering. 'I think that's long enough. Go and get some breakfast. We'll come for you if there's any change.'

'Is he going to get better?' she asked desperately.

'It's too early to say, but I'm hopeful,' the doctor told her. 'He came into our care very quickly after the on-slaught of the disease and once a lumbar puncture had confirmed meningitis we started him on immediate intra-venous injections of antibiotics, which are starting to take effect and fending off the septicaemia which is our biggest worry at the moment. If he can get through the next two days I will feel happier.'

He gave her a gentle push in the direction of the door. 'Now go and get that breakfast. You will do the man no favours if you're in a state of collapse when he needs you.'

Was there a curse on her? Claudia wondered as she forced down a slice of toast. First Jack had been taken from her and now the vicious fates had laid their hands on Lucas.

Strong, unbeatable Lucas, who would take the world on if he had to, had been laid low by a deadly virus that could have come from anywhere, although the neurological ward at Lizzie's did seem the likeliest place.

If she lost him too she would be finished. Her love for Jack Tomlin had been a tranquil, caring thing, but it was as nothing compared to the way she felt about Lucas.

A nurse from Intensive Care had just entered the restaurant and Claudia rose awkwardly to her feet, but the girl just smiled and joined the queue at the counter.

As she sank back onto the chair Claudia's heartbeat slowed down and she went back to nibbling the toast. As the doctor had said, she would be no use to Lucas if she became faint through lack of food.

'Shall I let Sophie know?' Oliver asked when he came back in the early afternoon. 'She and Dimitri are living in Greece now.'

'I don't know,' Claudia told him. 'I suggest we ask the doctor what he advises.'

'Dr Morrison is still maintaining a slight improvement,' he told them. 'You could probably notify his sister and warn her to be on standby for the time being,' and, turning to Claudia, he added, 'I think you should go home for a few hours.'

She shook her head. 'I can't bear to leave him. He might need me.'

'All right, but you must stay in the visitor's suite to-night. I believe that it isn't long since you sustained the leg fracture at Lizzie's.'

Claudia looked down at her leg and the long black skirt concealing the plaster. It seemed like a lifetime since she'd dressed to go out with Lucas.

Since then she'd gone through the torments of hell and by the looks of it would continue to do so for some time yet.

Every so often she was allowed to see him for a few minutes and that was the reason why she wouldn't budge. Lucas had to know that she was there, loving him, praying for him, and if the black outfit was becoming more creased by the minute and her pallor increasing at the same rate, she didn't care.

She and Oliver had been vaccinated and on the Monday morning the same facility was offered to the staff at Lizzie's where they had only just heard what had happened.

Marina Beauchamp came to visit him in her lunch-hour

and when Claudia saw her hovering outside the waiting room door she went to greet her, thinking as she did so that a short time ago her feelings towards the woman would have been vastly different from what they were today.

'I'm so terribly sorry,' Marina said. 'Lucas has been a good friend to Peter and I. My husband asked him to take care of us if anything happened to him and he has been wonderful. Lots of men would have taken that sort of commitment with a pinch of salt, but not Lucas. I do hope he will soon be well.

'I got engaged last week to an old school friend of mine and I was hoping that when we marry in a few weeks' time Lucas would give me away. But as things are at the moment I feel that the best thing is to postpone the wedding.'

'Recovery from meningitis can be reasonably quick once the process has begun,' the consultant told her. 'I should wait and see, if I were you.'

Wait! Claudia thought raggedly. That was all they could do...wait. She knew the walls and floor of the waiting room better than she knew her own face. Every crack in the ceiling. The number of panes in the window. How many seats there were. Which was the best vantage point for observing the comings and goings of the staff.

Oliver had gone home to shower and change when the doctor came to her finally and the look on his face told her that the limbo she'd been living in was nearly over.

'He's going to get better, Claudia,' he said. 'It's been touch and go, but the man's a fighter...and if I had someone like you waiting for me I think I'd be the same. Go and have a word with him and then I suggest that you go home and get some sleep, otherwise you'll be the next one to be hospitalised.'

'You looked exhausted,' Lucas said when she went to him. 'How long have you been here?'

'Claudia's been here ever since you were brought in,' a passing nurse told him.

He groaned. 'Why, Claudia, for goodness' sake? I was scared stiff you might get it.'

'Yes, I know you were. That was why you stood me up, wasn't it? But it would have been kinder to let me know you were ill. Do you remember what I said the first time they let me see you?' she asked gently.

'No. Should I?'

'It doesn't matter for now,' she told him with a weary smile. 'Just keep on improving. I'm going home to get out of these clothes and then maybe I might be able to sleep for a while, which is something I've been afraid to do in case…'

'The tiger popped his clogs?' he prompted quizzically.

Claudia shuddered. 'Don't say it! I can't bear to even think of it. I'll see you tomorrow, Lucas. Oliver will be in to see you later. We've been keeping each other company.'

'You have?' Dark brows rose.

'Well, yes. We had Sophie on standby and he and I have been supporting each other here.'

'I can see that the boot is well and truly on the other foot,' he said slowly. 'I owe you, Claudia.'

She shook her head. 'The only thing you owe me is to get well…and your friend Marina is anxious for that too, for various reasons. One of them being that she wants you to give her away when she gets married in the very near future.'

On the way back to the apartment Claudia thought ruefully that it wasn't a good idea to tell a man that you loved him

when he was semi-conscious—not if one wanted the relationship to progress.

Lucas didn't remember her confessing how much he
meant to her in those desperate moments when his life had
hung in the balance. So where did she go from there? If
she were to tell him now it might seem as if she were
doing it out of compassion and, knowing him as she did,
he would take a poor view of that.

Leave it, she told herself. You will see things in a different light when you've slept.

When she'd gone Lucas lay gazing thoughtfully into space.
He was aware that he had nearly died. There had been a
time when he'd been able to feel himself slipping towards
the dark passage that would have taken him...where? To
a place from which there was no coming back, that was
for sure.

But someone or something had halted that downward
slide and he'd found the will to fight back. In normal circumstances his own strength of character had always over-
come the difficulties that came his way, but this had been
in a different dimension. The power had been taken out of
his hands and he'd been helpless, until...?

The memory was there on the edge of his mind but he
couldn't quite take hold of it. There was a wall in front of
it and until it disappeared he wouldn't know.

It was humbling to think that while he'd been fighting
for life, his beautiful golden girl had been there for him,
along with the brother that he'd sometimes thought didn't
care.

Being in a position of dependency was not his favourite
mode. He liked to be in control. But there was something
oddly comforting in knowing that they'd cared enough to

wait through the long hours while he'd clawed his way back to recovery.

He would like to know what had been in Claudia's mind during that time. Had she felt beholden to stay because they were acquaintances and she wasn't sure if his younger siblings would be there for him? Or because she'd become involved through his non-appearance on the Saturday night and felt she couldn't back off?

There was another question he wanted to ask himself, but wasn't sure if he could cope with the answer that came up. Not today, anyway. Maybe tomorrow. And, turning his head into the pillow, he slept.

CHAPTER ELEVEN

IT WAS the last Saturday in May and the day of Marina Beauchamp's wedding to her old schoolfriend, Dennis Tyler. It was also the day after Claudia's notice at St Elizabeth's had expired and the day that a recuperating Lucas was to give the bride away.

He had been discharged from the hospital two days earlier with strict instructions to live at a slower pace until he was fully recovered, and to Claudia's surprise he seemed to be prepared to do just that.

'For once in my life I'm going to take time to look around me,' he'd told her. 'You remember I once said that I've scarcely had time to notice the seasons changing, so busy am I? Well, for a little while I'm going to allow myself that pleasure…and more.'

Claudia had wondered whimsically how long that state of affairs would last. Lucas was too much a man of action to be idle for long. She'd also wondered if the 'and more' part of it would include herself.

They'd been together a lot during the time of his recovery but more as people drawn together in adversity than lovers. Lucas had never referred to those fraught moments when she'd told him how much she loved him, which made it seem that the only conclusions to be drawn from that were that either he'd been too ill for it to register, or he was adopting the approach of least said, soonest mended.

It was incredible to think that with Marina safely out of the way their relationship hadn't progressed any further, but there was a stubbornness inside her that wouldn't let her do anything about it.

She had attended the fracture clinic at Lizzie's a couple of times, where she'd had the healing process of her broken bones checked by Miles Soper, and while she'd been there had been informed by a gloomy Robin that it was hellish without Lucas and herself on the unit.

Claudia had been surprised to receive an invitation to the wedding. When she'd informed Lucas he'd said, 'But of course you are coming to the wedding. I told Marina that I want you to be there when I finally hand over my two charges to their new keeper. It will mark a new era. For once in my life I'll be free to go my own way.

'Oliver is at last showing some signs of maturity. Sophie and her Dimitri are settling nicely in Greece and now Marina has found happiness.'

Claudia had listened in silence. If the situation was giving him pleasure, there was none in it for her. Not a word about them…their future…and she was damned if she was going to be the one to bring up the subject.

Her life was on hold. She'd left Lizzie's—mistakenly, she felt—and her future was in the same state as Lucas had once described his: shrouded in mist.

Where did she go from here? she asked herself as she waited for him to take her to the wedding. Maybe after today that would be it.

She was going to end up with lots of time on her hands if she didn't get another job soon. While he, once he was back in his usual slot, would be well and truly out of her orbit. There would be no situation where they might meet.

Her thoughts went back to the wedding. It was to be a very quiet affair, with only themselves, the bride and groom, the bride's son and a few friends present.

Peter was still making progress but had a long way to

go and, with the shadow of his illness hanging over them, a big wedding hadn't been considered.

Claudia had decided on a long-skirted dress of pale green silk with a wide-brimmed matching hat and the effect in her mirror was exactly what she wanted, just as long as she didn't look downwards to where one high-heeled cream shoe and one bare foot protruding from the plaster were on view.

This time there was no long, frustrating wait for someone who didn't turn up. He arrived on the dot, looking thinner but just as mesmeric as ever in a grey morning suit.

In that moment all Claudia's doubts and misgivings were swept aside by a great wave of thankfulness. Lucas was back to how he used to be. Nothing else mattered. There were tears in her eyes as she opened the door to him and he looked at her questioningly.

'What's wrong?' he asked urgently as she moved slowly backwards on the crutches.

She shook her head. 'Nothing.'

'You're weeping over nothing?'

'It was just an emotional moment, watching you get out of the car…alive and well after all those dark moments of despair when you were so ill.'

His eyes had darkened. 'Do I really mean that much to you, Claudia?' he asked in a low voice. 'I have remembered what you said to me that night when I was fighting for my life. It came back to me a few days later, but how could I hold you to something you'd said in a moment of extreme anxiety?

'How was I to know that it wasn't a desperate ploy to make me fight the meningitis? I didn't, and ever since I've been afraid to tell you how much I love you too, in case

I found that I was foisting myself onto a woman who had told me she cared for me out of pity.'

'Pity!' she breathed. 'That's the last emotion you would ever bring to life in me. Joy. Desire. Tenderness. Respect. I could name a thousand emotions that I've felt since meeting you, but never that.'

'So you did mean what you said?'

He was moving towards her and as his arms reached out for her she let the crutches fall away.

'Yes, of course I did. I love and adore you. You brought me to life again after losing Jack. I discovered that what I'd felt for him was just a gentle affection compared to my feelings for you.'

Lucas groaned. 'I've been so afraid of stepping into a dead man's shoes and not coming up to scratch. I can't believe I'm hearing this!'

Claudia laughed and it was a joyous sound. 'And I've been jealous as hell of Marina Beauchamp. You told me you had a commitment to her and I got it all wrong. What a pair of problem inventors we've been.'

'Not any more, my darling girl. From now on, nothing or no one will come between us. When I was expressing my delight at my new-found freedom the other day I wanted to tell you that there was one bond that I wanted to forge, rather than cast off, but I never dreamt that it would come about.

'Will you marry me, Claudia? Are you prepared to take on the urban tiger?'

Her smile was brighter than the sun in the sky. 'Yes. I'm prepared to take that risk, my darling, if you are willing to take on one of the nation's jobless.'

His hold on her tightened. 'Were you serious when you talked of going to work in the Third World?'

'It's something I've considered, yes.'

'Me too. Let's go together once we're married. There will always be children who need us, Claudia, and until we have some of our own that's where I'd like to spend some time. My contract at Lizzie's will be up in a few months. There would be nothing to stop us then.'

She nodded. 'Where you are I want to be, Lucas. Where you go, I want to go...for ever and always.'

'It's incredible to hear you say that,' he said huskily. 'I never thought that my golden girl would ever belong to me.'

As the clock on the wall behind them chimed he sighed. 'We have a wedding to go to and all I want at this moment is to make love to you!'

'We have all the rest of our lives to do that,' she said with soft laughter, 'but your friend Marina will only have this one wedding day—so if you'd like to pass me my crutches...'

READER SERVICE™

The best romantic fiction direct to your door

Our guarantee to you...

The Reader Service involves you in no obligation
to purchase, and is truly a service to you!

There are many extra benefits including a free
monthly Newsletter with author interviews,
book previews and much more.

Your books are sent direct to your door
on 14 days no obligation home approval.

We offer huge discounts on selected books
exclusively for subscribers.

Plus, we have a dedicated Customer Care team
on hand to answer all your queries on
(UK) 020 8288 2888
(Ireland) 01 278 2062.

MILLS & BOON®

Makes
any time
special

Enjoy a romantic novel from
Mills & Boon®

Presents...™ *Enchanted*™ TEMPTATION.

Historical Romance™ ⌁**MEDICAL
ROMANCE**™

MAT1

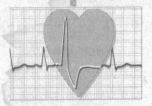

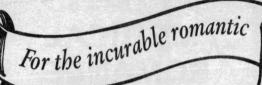